MURDER MAN

MURDER MAN

by

WILLIAM BOGART

Fiction House Edition published June 2022

isbn 978-1-64720-588-1

Fiction House Press
www.FictionHousePress.com

CHAPTER ONE

THE BUILDING was so old that the windows shuddered every time the BMT express shot by underground. It was on lower Fifth Avenue, near 23rd Street, in the garment and toy center of Manhattan. On the thirteenth floor a painter stood in front of the frosted glass door of suite 1037, and sadly shook his head at the obviously cheap grade lettering. The door's inscription, like fine print on a tombstone, read: *Moe Martin—Literary Agent* and just below, *John J. Saxon*—Literary Consultant. With sudden zeal the painter began to scrape off the lower legend. When it had disappeared completely, he blocked in new words. These were in letters of bold and elegant style and said: *Johnny Saxon, Private Investigator. I Never Seelp.* With a final deft stroke the painter finished, and stepped back. He nodded appreciatively, turned, and walked away.

Inside office A of the two-office suite, Moe Martin, wearing a rumpled suit, sat at a battered roll-top desk, his shiny bald head inclined as his bloodshot eyes pored over a wilted manuscript. In wire baskets on Moe's desk, and in piles a foot high on either side of the baskets were similar shop-worn scripts. Book-length tomes were piled three feet high on the floor. Dust had long ago sifted gently over their yellowing pages in a beautiful silver sheen. Dust had also settled over the broad windows in a murky haze of nickel. There was no carpet on the floor, and the only other furniture consisted of two old chairs and a wooden table. The table was burdened with manuscripts also and it was a little knock-kneed due to the fact that careless people had been sitting on it. But the walls of the office were classical.

On the south wall was pinned an authentic letter from the editor of *Dynamite Detective* saying that if a client cared to do an extensive revision on a story entitled *Murder in the Battery* he would reconsider it. Below this was pasted an envelope on which Moe had scrawled "Contained check for One Hundred and Eighty Bucks"; there were other such mementoes: book-jackets bearing the imprint of defunct companies, snapshots of Moe with his arm around an editor, several rough-paper pulp magazine covers, each of them with the name *Johnny Saxon* splashed in big letters across the front.

Moe himself, the loneliest literary agent in New York, did not want to go back to wrapping packages in a department store—a job he had gladly relinquished twelve years ago—and he toiled with diligent and infinite patience over each dog-eared manuscript—searching fruitlessly for a genius. Moe obtained these rhetorical gems from all over the country through the device of advertisements in a writer's trade journal. The reason he had so many was that he couldn't afford stamps to send them back.

In his advertisement Moe could not offer the inducements nor boast the success of high pressure agents (who charged reading fees up to five dollars for every short story) so he charged no fee. He reasoned that this wily method would bring him more scripts and thus enhance his chance of finding talent. This, of course, was a mistake, because Moe didn't know talent when he saw it. He was an emotional sponge. He could lose himself in any narrative, no matter how bad, and biting his fingernails through to the end, wipe his eyes when he finished and start the next one. He read day and night. And, on a few fine rare occasions he had actually stumbled upon authors he could peddle. But as soon as they had sold five or six stories—and were foxy enough to realize that Moe's critical ability was short—they sailed away from him into the arms of the Robber Barons who were ready to grasp to their agency bosom any name that appeared in print more than four times. Moe would only sigh when this happened, and continue his endless hunt—the search for a loyal author.

Moe was of medium height, wide-set, with a large chest, and a fringe of dark, wiry black hair around his bald pate. He was a professional optimist and, like a stray dog, everybody's friend. People thought him the happiest man alive. But that was not true. There were moments when he suffered acute agony. This morning, for instance, he knew that unless a miracle occurred, the end was in sight. Moe had eaten no breakfast.

Listlessly, he cast aside the script. He leaned back in his swivel chair, folding his hands behind his head. He thought of bacon and eggs, oatmeal with cream, sausages. He rubbed his tired eyes and stretched. From over the transom in the other office there came a profound silence. But now the hall door opened and a large, unpleasant young man entered.

"Ah, good morning, Louie," Moe said.

Louie's face was bloated with anger. There was a bundle of manuscripts under his arm and he dumped them on the desk. His legs apart, he stood a little forward on the balls of his feet. He was trembling. He pulled off cloth gloves. He let them drop to the floor. His narrowed eyes were riveted upon Moe.

Moe stirred uneasily. "Is there—anything wrong?" He felt an icy chill dart down his spine.

Louie Hart had been, off and on, the office messenger. At twenty-one he was over-grown, thick-set, and he possessed very little imagination. His was a realistic world. He wore a heavy black coat and a scarf, but was hatless, and there was snow in his ugly, kinky hair. His eyes were dark and close-set. His cheeks were splotchy with color. He moved silently forward, reached out to cuff Moe across the face. Moe ducked and went over backwards in the swivel chair. He climbed to his feet. Louie gave him a shove with the flat of his hand. Now his trembling lip twisted, and he moved his hand to the open breast of his top coat.

"You dirty rats. You and Johnny . . . took me for a ride, didn't you? Go *ahead and deny it!* You got everything out of me you wanted. Got everything but a written confession, didn't you?" His low, husky voice dripped venom. "Now Johnny turns cop. Just at this time—he turns cop!"

Moe felt sick. Louie was an unarrived author from the East Side. His brother was a petty but dangerous racketeer associated until recently with a murder syndicate in Brooklyn. Louie had wandered into Moe's office (he'd read the ads) months ago. His jargon had been so pictorial, his idle commentary about criminals so obviously authentic that Johnny Saxon (who for the past two years had been Moe's partner) had given him a temporary job as messenger, while at night he collaborated with him on stories. They did six. They bristled with fact, but they were too brutal to print. Even though they never sold, Johnny swore by them. Louie, meanwhile, dazzled by Johnny's pulp magazine fame, had gradually poured out his cold black heart.

He'd related one incident after another about actual cases of murder. He liked to talk, and flattering himself that he was Johnny's side-kick, he had told too much; he was naming real names, places and dates: material that any D. A. in the country would sell his soul to get. And now, just a week ago, the murder syndicate had been broken wide open. Some of the gang had taken it on the lam; others were already behind bars. Louie's brother—notorious Les Hart—had been one of the first to be slapped into a cold cell in the Tombs.

Louie was breathing hard. "The D. A.'s been working on the murder mill for months. This was the angle, wasn't it? He had Johnny Saxon work on me. You two were broke and you sold me out. Johnny will be a surprise witness—and Les will go to the hot seat! You two poison rats got me to talk. Begged me to talk. *We're your friends, Louie!*"

"Look, kid, we——"

"Don't tell *me!*" He began to back up. "What are you doin' tellin' me! My brother's mouthpiece called me, see? He said it was in the *Times* that Johnny was turning cop. Then I come here and it's on the door. I think maybe it's some mistake. But it's on the door."

His face was acid.

"Listen," Moe said.

"You might have at least paid me my salary, you dirty, ratting cheap-skates! For two months I trot your stinking stories all over town. I even pay my own subway fare. That's gratitude! I even loan you money sometimes. You cheap damn heels!"

Moe gestured futilely. He'd begun to sweat.

"You're rats . . . dirty stinking *Judas*-rats. You ain't going to pin nothin' on Les. You maybe think so. You and that lard-bellied, big talkin' D. A.. But you ain't, see . . . ?"

Moe's bloodshot eyes widened. Louie had reached inside his coat and brought out a small automatic.

"Louie—you dope!"

"Oh, no. I ain't a dope. I got my friends to think of! My friends come first, see?" He was backed up tight against the wall. "Just stand there . . . stand there pretty-like." He was shaking from head to foot, and he brought the gun up in his hand. It was wobbling, but he aimed it at Moe's chest.

Moe began to melt like butter. His hands were like windmills. He shifted from one foot to the other.

"Louie, listen—just listen for a minute! I'll tell you—"

"You ain't ever going to tell anything," Louie said. "I'm going to——"

Just then there was the clattering roar of an alarm clock.

The clock rang shrilly, incessantly in the adjoining office. In there the windows were even dustier, and there were two cardboard clothes-hampers, an electric plate with a small, nicked coffee pot on it—and two iron cots, the worse for wear. On one of these cots slept a tall, thin young man. One pajama-ed leg was flung out of the covers, and his iron-gray hair was tousled. The alarm clock kept ringing. He groped out, turned it off. Then Johnny Saxon sat up straight, yawning.

He looked around for a cigarette, found a long butt, unwrinkled it, and put it in his mouth. He lit up. He felt like hell. He'd gone to bed with the blues and woke up with them. Last week he'd hocked his little radio, and in the night he missed its tinny melodies. He looked at the icicles on the window, and at the falling snow. Winter in Manhattan. What a swell title, he thought. Kind of sad and beautiful. He puffed at the cigarette. Kind of tender—and peaceful.

The door was ruthlessly kicked open, and Louie Hart stood framed in the doorway with a gun. Johnny stared incredulously.

"So *this* is the way you've been living," Louie said. "Why, you two fakes! I thought you told me you were staying at the Astor on a due bill."

"It ran out," Johnny said. "What do you want us to

do—sleep in Washington Square?" He pinched out the cigarette butt. "Hey, there's a great title—*I Slept in Washington Square*."He crossed his legs. He was wearing polka dot pajamas.

For a moment Louie regarded Johnny in the awe of idol worship. Then he sobered.

"Stand up, Johnny. I'm going to give it to you standing up."

"Give me *what?* You mean with that gun? Jesus—is it loaded? Where'd you swipe it?"

"Never mind that."

"Put it in your pocket and see what happens," Johnny said.

"No, Johnny, I'm sorry. I'm really sorry." Louie stood with the gun gripped in his big fist.

Johnny kicked out one long leg, and climbed from the bed. Barefoot, he started across the room. On the way he stopped to extract a thumbtack from the sole of his foot. Then he suddenly reached over and knocked the gun from Louie's hand. The movement was quick, deft. Louie stooped to get it, and Johnny lifted his knee. Louie straightened up without the gun. He was sweating, and he grinned sheepishly.

"You were going to knee me, huh, Johnny?"

"I was going to kick you inside out," Johnny said. "Try again now. Pick up that gun."

"You won't——"

"Pick it up."

Louie bent his huge overcoated body and Johnny kicked him on over Louie sat on the floor, stuffing the gun in his pocket.

"Hell, I was joking, Johnny."

"Sure," Johnny said, "heh, heh."

He strode into the outer office. Moe, numb and dazed, was collecting himself. He sponged sweat from his bald head.

"Where's my orange juice?" Johnny said. "In fact, where's breakfast?"

Louie came in looking sorry about the whole thing. He and Moe exchanged a glance. Moe laughed nervously to show that never, at any time, had he been actually scared. Much. He slapped Louie on the back a little too hard.

"You've got us wrong kid," he said.

"Breakfast," Johnny said, "that's the thing." His eyes roved past the hall door, then came creeping back. He studied the freshly painted letters transparent through the glass. He gave Moe a withering look, walked to the door, and jerked it open. He read the pronouncement, opened his hand and let the door close. He leaned back against it, folding his arms.

"So you've done it?"

"You didn't *know?*" Louie asked.

But Johnny was watching Moe.

"Damn it," Moe said, "I'm hungry. The last decent ghost writer we had committed suicide—the coward—and I haven't had a single client selling stories! Even if I had, what's ten percent of sixty dollars!"

"Six," Louie said soberly.

"Johnny," Moe said dramatically, "we haven't even got dough for breakfast!"

"To hell! Didn't *any* of the manuscripts come in with return postage attached?"

"No. Not even a lousy two cent stamp," Moe said. "I don't know what's happened to my reputation."

Johnny walked thoughtfully across the office, pushed a pile of manuscripts off the table, and hoisted himself up. His legs dangled glumly.

"You used to be one of the best private cops in New York," Moe went on hopefully. "There must be a few people that still remember. I thought you and me and"—he glanced at Louie—"and the kid could work together. I could continue as a literary agent——"

"As a what?"

"Never mind. I could continue. No matter how broke I am, Johnny, I always have my friends."

"Sure—where are they now?"

"Anyway, I could do the clerical work for the detective agency on the side. The kid can be a spare gum-shoe."

"Me a cop!" Louie said.

Johnny glanced over at him. "It isn't like being a cop.

Some private detectives are the biggest crooks you ever saw."

"That's better," Louie said.

"I thought it'd please you."

"Then it's okay?" Moe asked.

"Did I say it was?"

"Well, no but——"

"I want to think," Johnny said. "What a stinking way to make a living! Helluva Friday morning, isn't it?" His eyes came up and lingered on the detective magazine covers on which his name was so gaudily splashed, and there was just a little ache in his heart. "That's me up there." He nodded toward the covers. "Prince of the pulps. Four, five hundred a week—on good weeks," he added.

"We must make the best of life," Moe said.

"What are you—the Blue Fairy! I can't take that poison this morning, Uncle."

Depressed, Louie sat down. He opened his coat and heaved a sigh.

Johnny watched him bleakly. He thought of the past. Five years ago he'd had his own private detective agency, all the business he could handle, a growing reputation, a smart-cracking girl assistant (just like in Dashiel Hammett), and on all this he had walked out. Simply because he had written and sold a story. He wrote other stores, and presently he found himself a thumping success—in the rough papered pulp magazines.

He learned formula, bought an electric typewriter, and ground out words by the ream for the fast action magazines. He wrote furiously, sometimes up to ten thousand words in a single day. In a year he was the most prolific writer in America. He started a whole new school of pulp writing. He was imitated by half the professionals in the business. Once, at his peak, he counted fifteen different pulps on the newsstands in the same month that contained his work. All because he'd written emotion instead of bang-bang. It was only natural. He was a romantic guy. He was—for a time—the boy wonder. It came to a point where he either had to graduate into the slicks, or burn out. He did neither.

After three years he simply stopped writing. The business had lost its kick for him. His stuff went stale. When he tried to write stories in which he no longer believed, it wasn't the same. After a few rejections, he had the good sense to quit. All he had left was the immortality of those three years.

He had been living up to every penny, and when the pennies stopped he came to see Moe Martin. Moe suggested Johnny join him as literary consultant. He argued that his name would bring in money from amateurs who imagined a collaboration course with a professional was just the magic they needed to put them on the royal road to Rupert Hughes. The idea flopped because Johnny and Moe suddenly discovered there wasn't racketeer enough in either of them to bleed money out of the little people who wrote such heart-rending letters and sent in their rumpled, worn five and ten dollar bills. It'd be easier to commit murders for a living, or break labor union strikes. Something simple.

Johnny next tried a come-back via the ghost writer scheme. He'd plot stories, put his name on them, and the ghosts would do the work, putting in (he hoped) the spark of life that Johnny's fiction had lost. This worked fine, but the ghosts were for the most part rum-sodden hacks, and once a check came in, they'd disappeared. One committed suicide in a sordid Greenwich Village bar after a four-day bout—he was sixty-three years old; another landed in a straight-jacket in Bellevue.

Now, at last, Johnny and Moe had come to the end of their wits.

"I put ads in the *World-Telegram*, *Times* and *Trib*," Moe said. "Each announces the *I Never Sleep* is again in existence—J. Saxon in the saddle."

"Where'd you get the dough?"

"I telephoned—told each paper to send its bill to J. Saxon."

"Thanks, Uncle."

Moe nodded toward the door. "The painter was an old fan of yours. He did the lettering on credit."

Johnny shrugged. He straightened the front of his pajama jacket, then he said: "Give me that gun, Louie.

A detective should have a gun." Louie handed up the gun and Johnny looked at it. "*Hell on Friday*," he reflected. He glanced up. "Hey, that's a swell title, you know it?"

The phone rang, dust flying from the bell box.

Johnny stared at Moe. They both looked at Louie. For a moment all three were petrified.

"For—for Christ sake answer it!" Johnny said.

"No, let it ring again. I want to listen to the sound."

Moe let it ring twice more, then he picked up the receiver. He was almost trembling.

"Moe Martin Literary Agency," he said with dignity. "Mr.—*who*—Mr. Joseph Rogers?" Moe's face lost color. "Yes, Mr. Rogers?" He held the phone against his chest. "It's Mr. Rogers." He spoke into the mouthpiece. Yes . . . the what? The—*I Never Sleep*—no, I'm sorry, there's no detective agency here by that—oh, *oh yes!* I —he's—he's right here!"

With shaking hands he gave Johnny the phone.

CHAPTER TWO

JOE ROGERS emerged from the elevator on the 40th floor, and walked down the hall. He was a tall man, lithe, and well-built; his eyes were gray. He had good shoulders. He also had a lousy cold. It had been snowing in New York for three days and the end was nowhere in sight. Joe reached a frosted glass door marked *Rogers Publishing Co.*, opened it, and went inside. The floor was black and white checkered linoleum, and the white leather furniture was modernistic. Several authors and a few shabby artists stood around hopefully, but the switchboard girl—behind her glass panel—spotted Joe and buzzed him through to the inner sanctums.

In the office corridor Joe felt better. Checks were signed Friday and it usually depressed him a little to know that so many people, so many families, depended on him. Today it haunted him. There were only a few legitimate publishers in this field, and Joe, one of the biggest, faced a crisis that threatened to wipe all twenty-two of his monthly magazines into absolute oblivion.

He walked down the hall now and office doors were open on both sides of him. He saw his editors and their assistants busy at their desks. Today was makeup day. All copy had to be edited and in the mail for the printers tomorrow. Each editor edited from two to six magazines and hired his own assistants. Joe himself seldom bothered to read scripts any more, as he had in the beginning when this now busy labyrinth consisted of only one shabby office, and the staff of Rogers Publishing Company numbered only himself and Hanna, editing a single detective magazine—which was now the best money-maker in their whole chain.

That had been six years ago. He had been a young man possessed of two things—an idea and friends. Today those friends who had backed him were his directors, and the idea had turned into an organization which paid a quarter of a million dollars a year forsto res alone. He'd come up fast, all right. "We need two offices . . . four . . . six——" Now he had half of the 40th floor. All of this while the rest of the world was in the throes of depression. But the end could come much, much faster!

He reached the length of the hall and entered his own spacious office. There was just one desk, highly polished, a thick black rug on the floor; the walls were panelled with oak. Of furniture, there was a divan, soft chair, and an elaborate phonograph-radio. On one wall there was a huge board where Hanna had put up all twenty-two of the covers for next month's issues. Her back was turned to him, and she was squeezing thumbtacks into the last cover. Outside the huge windows the Manhattan sky line was the color of slate, and snow was falling in soft, white crescents.

Joe shrugged off his coat and watched Hanna. He saw her yellow hair, the way it brushed her shoulders; her woolly dress, the beautiful silk-stockinged legs. She was standing on tip-toes, reaching up to the top of the board.

The radio was playing soft dance music, and it struck him all at once that there had always been Hanna. He didn't know what he would have done without her. She was his under-captain, and it was she, really, who ran the business: kept the printer's schedules, harassed tired editors for proof sheets, harangued the News Company for more distribution and better display placards on the newsstands and delivery trucks.

It was Hanna, too, who lunched with him; at the Pen & Pencil, at the Lexington, in the Automat when they were jammed for time; and they'd been together that beautiful Christmas Eve when they'd both worked so late—and afterward had gone to a night club . . . and then a whole crazy, giddy circuit of clubs, ending in her apartment. In her apartment, and the next morning, the way it had been, nothing quite real, but Hanna sitting up, her hair tousled, and saying:

"Joe, I guess you think I'm an awful tramp . . . I'll quit if you want."

"Like hell you'll quit!"

"I love you, Joe. You know, it's funny, I've loved you all these years. Don't let us be hurt by this. Let *us* be different.

"Sure, that's the way we'll be," he said, he *had* said, and kissed her. Then he went home, to his Great Neck home, and he had Christmas dinner with his wife. It was a big day because his wife had gotten out of the wheel-chair for the first time in four years . . . ever since that accident in the car the cold, sleety night she had started for Reno to get her divorce.

Hanna stepped back from the drawing board now, put her finger to her lips, held her head to one side and then the other, looking at the covers.

"Very elegant, Miss Carter."

She jumped.

"You—you might let a lady know. Did you have to scare me to death, Joe?"

"Sure, I'm *The Shadow*."

"What does he do?"

"He enters rooms and people can't see him."

He stuffed a cigarette between his lips, threw one leg over the edge of his desk, hoisted himself up, and lit the cigarette. Hanna was watching him, her lips glistening wet-red; her eyes a lovely cool green. She had high, immobile cheek bones. "Covers are all made up, eh?" Joe said. "They look good. About two hundred percent better than last month's batch."

"I made some slight changes in the art department," Hanna admitted.

He glanced down at the cigarette, then gazed thoughtfully at the square, gaudy covers of his magazines—magazines printed not on slick, glossy paper but rough fibre wood pulp.

"Those covers'll increase sales," Joe said. "But we'll still be dying, Hanna." He nodded. "Take *Lightning Detective Stories* there—the October returns came in like a wet rain. It sold thirty thousand copies. At a dime a throw, the price of the wood pulp up, the British market shot out from under us, and the large print order we had on it—I don't have to tell you it's losing money. We've either got to peddle forty-five thousand on that book or call it a day—a dark, murky day. A day of inter-office weeping."

She gazed at the magazine's cover picture: a burly gunman was emerging from a bullet-riddled car, his left arm protectively about a girl, a blazing gun in his right hand.

"I think maybe that's too conservative."

"Sure it is." Joe agreed. "But never mind . . . cast your lovely eyes on *Superior Crime Tales*. It rolled up a grand total of thirty-three thousand. No hits, no runs, no profits. In fact ten thousand less than in September. And the Fall is supposed to be boom months!"

"Yah," Hanna said glumly.

"Take *Western Excitement* there," Joe went on, "forty thousand; *Bunk House Yarns* came home with a plurality of twenty thousand—we'll kill that one. Call around town to the other publishers—ask if anybody wants to buy the title cheap."

"How cheaply?"

"Fifty bucks for that masthead would be robbery."

"Consider it sold," Hanna said. She followed his anxious eyes to the cover board. "How are the love mags going?"

"Better. Thank God. *Cinderella Stories* is actually collecting dimes hand over heart, and *Romantic Girl* is holding her own."

He stopped suddenly, pinching out the cigarette. Hanna had fetched a whiskey decanter. Joe poured the drinks himself.

"Baby," he said, "we're going to fight. We've got one last chance. I've needled editors all along the line and the issues going to bed today should be a helluva lot improved." He paused. "The only trouble is—people grab the first title in sight and end up with a Sontag dud. Gypped! You put quality on the presses—and then it gets lost in a newsstand haystack. But I'm sticking to quality. We're going to rush out two new titles. *War Romances* is one. A hundred and twenty-eight pages. Penny-a-word budget."

"There's hungry guys that'll work for less."

"I know. But I'll keep this house's rates up to a cent a word if it kills us."

"It will."

"All right. But until it does, we're playing it straight."

"What's the second title?"

"Another cinderella book—*Gallant Love*—with a heavy masculine angle—cop and soldier heroes, a few period stories, the same honey-sweet gals. Get Miss Hayworth to edit it."

"But she's only a reader!"

"I know. Promote her. Give her a purpose in life. Tell her to stand by for some of the best copy a pulp's ever been able to print."

"Hey, pop, I'm beginning to smell terrific ambition!" She looked at him "You sound just like you did that first year when we——"

"I know! I'm waking up. Too late, perhaps, but—listen, do you know what name is going to go across the cover of *War Romances* and *Gallant Love?* Do you? Do you know?"

"What is this—a monologue?"

"No, you don't know. Honey, I've been in there pitching. "He strode around behind the desk, opened the drawer and triumphantly lifted out a huge manilla envelope postmarked New Orleans. From the envelope he extracted—as though it were on silver paper—two thick manuscripts. "Ten-thousand-word novelettes," he said. "Two of them."

"So what? Tons of script arrives every half-hour by mail, pony express messenger, dog sled . . ."

"Look, beautiful—at the by-line. See the lovely by-line?"

"Dulcy Dickens! *Dulcy*——"

"Yeah, sweet. In person. Do you know who she is? I mean—*exactly?*"

"Well, she writes for Sam Sontag——"

"She did. *Did.* Past tense. Like in high school. Do you know what friend Sontag was paying her? One-half cent a word! Can you see it? In the four months she's been writing, she's become the hottest thing that ever hit the pulps. She's a phenomenon! She only writes for the pulps because she's an amateur. Why, this girl could be writing for slicks, doing plays best sellers, movies! But she doesn't know that yet. She free-lances. Some body told her to try the pulps. She has no agent."

"Writes period stuff, doesn't she?"

"Yeah, and modern war. Escape stories. Like that. Do you know how I got those two novelettes?"

"You tell me, master mind."

"I sent one of our writers—who occasionally sells Sontag a story—to have lunch with the Sontag editor who's been buying Dulcy's stuff. It all came out then—like dirty laundry. I found out she was in New Orleans. Living in the French quarter. But her address is unknown—she gets all mail General Delivery—and if she has a phone, it must be a private listing or under some other name. Anyhow, I put a personal in all the papers down there asking her to call me. And after a while, she did."

"What was she like?"

"Have you met Yvette?"

"That's a slogan. But go on."

"She talks like Yvette sings."

"Synonym for French, feminine and lovely."

"She called on the phone, and I asked her for stories—"

"And she sang you one!"

"No. She just said 'Why certainly, Mr. Rogers, I'd be *glad* to write you a story . . . .' Five days later—I had them sent to my house—these came air mail. Why, she must have written twenty thousand words in four days!"

"Or sent you rejects."

"She doesn't know what the word means."

"Have you—by any chance—*read* these masterpieces?"

"Of course, and they're terrific! Plot, writing, style, timing. Even characterization!"

"That alone should revolutionize the business," Hanna said.

"Hanna, pet. She's like nothing we've ever had. She's as prolific as any of our hacks—but *fresh.* Her sentences are crisp and new. Her writing stimulates you."

"Joe, forgive me for having a long memory. But people in this biz used to say the same thing, using the very same adjectives—about a guy named Johnny Saxon. A pretty swell guy as memory serves."

"All right. Okay. And for a time it was true. Which reminds me—I've got to call Saxon. He's going to be the biggest part of my fight against Sontag. To get back to Dulcy Dickens, though."

"Do we *have* to, Pop?"

"No—but we'd better. Our distributor told me that without any prodding news dealers are featuring covers that have her name on them. She's written only for Sontag, but the distributor said we have to have her. Not since the Horatio Alger craze has a single writer been so important to the industry. The beauty of it is, Sontag doesn't know it yet!"

"But this girl, like Johnny Saxon, she might——"

"She's good for another year yet isn't she? Or even two!"

"So?"

"So I sent her a check for these two stories and told her to hop the first train for New York." He gulped his drink, poured another one, looking very smug. "She arrives at Grand Central—midnight tonight. I'm going to have Johnny Saxon's agency meet her and sign her to an exclusive contract to us."

"Pop—how come you aren't doing this yourself?"

He held out his hand.

"I ask you, would it look right for me, a publisher, to——"

"Not if it ever got out—because it's a dirty, lousy trick!"

"What do you mean? Sontag's been paying her a half-penny! He's a louse, a crook, and three kinds of a dirty son. I'd have absolutely no compunction about killing Sontag—and I mean cold-blooded murder, baby; so if you think it hurts my already bad conscience to steal a writer from him—hell, I'm doing the girl a favor!"

"Oh, certainly, you are! The slicks would pay her— if what you say is true—ten times your rate, but you're doing her a *favor*!"

He stuck another cigarette in his mouth. "That part." He lit up. "That's business. You savvy business, don't you gorgeous? And you know I'm no robber. I'll start her at a cent, keep jumping the price until it's four cents a word. Pulps haven't paid that in years—but, by God, I'll pay it to her——"

"Sure, as soon as her name sugars the public to your covers—and nets you half a million or so. Gee, Joe, you're generous!"

"Five cents a word then! I'm no Shylock. In a few weeks I'll pay her five cents a word. Even for the commas and exclamation points. And if she does not like that, I'll pay her six cents, and I'll include the periods."

"You won't though, Mr. Publisher, you know that, don't you? You're dreaming. Because nothing's *that* good any more. But please continue. Don't mind me. Just keep talking."

"No, I'm through talking. Here—take these Dulcy Dickens'. One each for the two new titles. Be sure she's prominent on the covers. You won't have time to get cover pictures made up, so give the first issues a Scribner's format."

"Ah, dignity!"

"And prestige."

"Yah—but I never thought I'd see the day an author's name would replace cover pictures. You'll have artists picketing the building—*Dulcy Dickens Unfair to Art!*"

Joe Rogers wasn't listening. He lifted a whiskey pony, spoke almost into it. "Sam Sontag's been bleeding and sucking the life out of this business long enough. Before I'm through, there's going to be hell to pay. For him and that gangster distributor of his, both."

"You mean Jasper Ward?"

"Yeah. A racketeer. The racketeers finally moved in on us. We've taken it over two years. Now it's war to the death." He gulped the drink. "Go on, beat it, baby. I've got to phone Johnny Saxon. He used to be a good cop—and he knows this business backwards. Between us we'll stir up trouble for Sontag—or die trying." He fished a newspaper clipping from his pocket and moved to the phone. Hanna was at the door, and Joe looked up. "Whatever you do, keep those two new titles quiet. If it gets out, some quickie house'll copy 'em and get them

—or reasonable facsimiles thereof—on the stands before we can. And there we'll be—holding the bag! What a cut-throat business!"

Hanna left, and in a few moments Johnny Saxon was on the telephone.

"I'm coming over to see you, Johnny," Joe said. "I think we can do business. It's about Sam Sontag." With his left hand he poured a drink from the decanter. "Yeah—Sam Sontag, the dirty rat. Remember him?"

CHAPTER THREE

SAM SONTAG returned to his office from lunch that day in a fine frame of mind. His paunchy stomach was digesting mackerel, and as he stepped from the elevator a toothpick moved contentedly up and down between his lips. He was a square-set man, and he wore a black felt hat the brim of which was too large. His hair was lemon in color but at his temples it had whitened. Because he disliked wasting his valuable time in a barber shop (no one was more conscious of his importance than himself) he almost always needed a hair-cut. As a result his side-burns resembled downy tufts. He was forty-six, ruddy-cheeked, and his eyes were small and dark. He strode across the Sontag Publishing Company's small, cramped reception room and viewed coldly the handful of artists and writers seated on a narrow wooden bench. "See here, men," he said, "the checks won't be signed until five o'clock."

He was at once sorry that he had paused to give the information because it enabled an artist to corner him.

The artist was a very old man and he trembled in the presence of anyone so great as Sontag. Because it embarrassed him to ask his question within hearing of those who sat on the bench, the old man's eyes watered with nervousness as he began to speak.

"Mr. Sontag—I'm sorry to bother you. I know that you—ah—your company, rather, always pays on publication. But two of my covers have been okayed by the art department and, I—I——"

"You what, my man? Speak up!"

"I—just wondered if—" the old man smiled and embarrassed tears ran down his face, embarrassing him more. "Since all the other companies pay on acceptance, if—just this once—I couldn't get some cash on my work. I——"

"If you feel that way," Sontag snapped, "I suggest you work for the other companies." He paused. "Unless I'm mistaken, your art's gone to pot, and no one else would have you. Isn't that true?"

"Well, I—my family, you see——"

"*I'm* generous enough to give you work. And now the thanks I get is to have you pestering me for an advance. The answer is 'no'. If I gave it to you, I'd have to give it to everyone else."

"But, Mr. Sontag, my wife's sick, and——"

Sontag dug into his pocket. "Here. Here's five dollars. This is a personal loan. Now get out."

"Yes, sir."

Sontag slammed into the inner office corridor. *I'm a sucker*, he thought. *They think I'm easy.* But that was the trouble one ran into when one paid only a third of the normal price for art work.

It was that way with a good many other things. Jasper Ward, the distributor with whom he was affiliated, insisted that all production costs be cut to the bone. The Sontag publications were out for a quick, cheap monoply of the business. Theirs were the gaudiest, crudest magazines on the stands. They employed non-union printers, used the worst grade paper, and Sontag obtained literary matter in every crooked way he knew. He bought old reprints at three and five dollars a story and pawned them off on the public—mixed with low priced new stories—as all new material. In Sontag's chain there were now thirty magazines, and new ones were being added every week.

Sontag glanced into the vast room where there were some thirty desks at which all of his editors worked. Heavy green metal lamp shades shone down and everyone was industriously at his place. Sontag turned into his own private office. It was small with a bookcase against one wall, two leather chairs, and a desk. The publisher took off his wide-brimmed black hat and hung it on a hook. He pulled his arms out of his coat and dropped it into a chair.

His one large window looked out on a court, and he stood there, chewing the toothpick, when the door opened and his secretary came in. She had a batch of stories in her hand, and she laid them on the desk. Sontag turned and regarded her.

She was a tall, slim girl, with olive skin, and long black hair done up in a smart coiffure. Her eyes were flashing black, and her lips glistened bright orange-red. Over her mellon-smooth hips she wore a dark green dress, the hem of which broke just above her shapely knees. She nodded toward the stories.

"These have all been okayed. An hour's editing will fix them. I wrote the authors that they had to be staff re-written and all but two agreed—because of the rewriting—to sell for twenty dollars a script."

"That's a third of a cent a word, isn't it, Miss Leigh?"

"It comes to about that," Kay Leigh said. "And George Howie called—he's that sub-editor at Rogers Publications."

"Yes, I know. One of our boys contacted him last month. What'd he have to report?"

Kay glanced at her notes. "Joe Rogers is rushing out two new magazines—*Gallant Love* and *War Romances*. Scribner's format."

"What an idea!" Sontag said. "It eliminates cover art!"

Kay nodded, her dark eyes watching the lemon-haired publisher. "Both mags are going to press with Dulcy Dickens on the cover."

"How did Rogers get her! Why, the crook!"

"She's a fee-lance writer, isn't she?"

"Yes. I guess so. . . . Tell our boys to get out two new magazines—duplicates—same titles—same format. We've got three or four Dickens' on hand. Slap her across the cover of both."

"But——"

"Outside of Dickens, fill the magazine with reprints. Get a rush print order. We'll be on the stands two days before Rogers can possibly get his copies out. Get Jasper Ward on the phone. Tell him we want display placards on *Gallant Love* and *War Romances*."

"Mr. Ward called half an hour ago," Kay said. "He's on his way over now." She started for the door.

"Wait a minute," Sontag said.

She stopped. "There was an old gentleman here asking to see Dulcy Dickens I told him that——"

"Never mind that," Sontag rasped. "What's the price going to be on Rogers' new books?"

"Dime."

"All right. Throw ours on the stands for a nickel. We'll lose money, but not nearly as much as him, and it'll kill him dead. He won't get a sale! He's almost on the rocks as it is. This'll cost him seven or eight thousand dollars in production costs alone. If we put out a hundred thousand print order it won't nick us more than eight hundred."

"But Mr. Sontag, *no* pulp sells for less than ten cents! During the depression there were a few, but——"

"I don't give a damn! Don't you see the point? If we drive Rogers out of business we inherit his market. Get to it now. We'll work tonight. I want dummy copies made up. By damn, by the time Rogers hits the stand with those titles of his we'll sue him for infringement—just to give him another little headache!"

"Okey doke," Kay said. Her smooth, dark-skinned face showed no emotion. "What about George Howie?"

Sontag felt expansive. "Send that louse twenty-five bucks. Tell him to keep up the good work!"

Jasper Ward arrived ten minutes later. He opened the door of Sontag's office and walked in. He stood against it, one foot propped behind him. He wore a dark hat over his white, thinly-chiseled face; his eyes were a strange light-colored gray. He wore a black shirt, and a yellow tie. There were heavy rings on his slim, tapering fingers, and from his coat lapel there was the smell of jasmine. He'd deposited his topcoat outside. He stood against the door, flipping a key in his hand, watching Sontag. His voice was low and smooth.

"I picked you up when you were on your can," he said. "The Federal Government ran you out of the toy business, and you were story editor of a two-bit independent studio in Hollywood."

Sontag looked up, puzzled.

Jasper Ward's voice flowed on. "We're partners in this racket . . . and we split the proceeds."

"So what, Jasp?"

"So you've been taking me down the line, you rat!" He strode to the desk, lifted Sontag by his vest, jerked him forward. "I just got your quarterly statement." He reached inside his coat, dropped the statement on the desk. With his other hand he kept hold of Sontag. "Thirty grand for four months! What do you think I'm playing for—marbles?"

"I swear to God, Jasp, those returns are right!"

Ward shoved the other back into the swivel chair. He adjusted his yellow tie, shoved back his hat. He was a man of thirty-seven, his eye-brows plucked, a yellow handkerchief in his breast pocket. There were lifts in the heels of his shoes that gave his slender body balance.

"You gave me a dirty deal," he said, "and I'll blow your heart out. Nobody ever gets the second chance to gyp me!"

"I swear to God——"

"Leave God out of it. I know you backwards, you yellow, cheating little dog. I want a new accounting. And there's something else."

"Yes?" Sontag quavered.

"I've had a report from news dealers. There's a new trend. It can make or break a dozen magazines."

"I—I hadn't heard."

"What have you been doing! We've been in business two years and we haven't bankrupted a single competitor yet! Where the hell are you? Asleep! The new trend is Dulcy Dickens. Some skirt from New Orleans. You've had her in all your books. Now Kay tells me that Joe Rogers——"

"I heard about that."

"Well, put it to a stop! Get her exclusively if you have to walk barefoot to New Orleans to do it. Iron-clad contract. Third of a cent a word."

"But I've been paying her a half!"

"Don't argue with me! You're guaranteeing her an income. She'll sign up—or by God, I'll see that she doesn't sign with anybody else! Trend is everything in the pulps. Do I have to tell you how to run your business?"

"I'll get Kay to write Dulcy right away," Sontag said.

"See that you do. Or I'll throw you out of this company on your face." Ward lifted a carefully tailored cuff and glanced at a delicate gold wrist watch. "I've got a date. Some of the murder syndicate boys have a chance of getting out on bail . . ." He looked up, his light-gray eyes icy. "You get some work done, fathead!"

"Sure," Sontag said feebly.

CHAPTER FOUR

JOHNNY SAXON sat on Moe's desk, watching the handsome, hard-jawed Joe Rogers as he talked. Moe Martin and Louie Hart sat back on the little table which, its legs more knock-kneed than ever, was on the verge of collapse. Snow fell past the window in huge white blobs, and now and then the thunder of the BMT subway, far underground, shook loose one of the icicles that hung outside. Rogers moved to get up.

"So that's it," he said. "I want Sontag's business checked from beginning to end. I'm sure that somewhere along the line we'll run into something that's outside the law. No legitimate organizations could get out books so cheaply. I want you to conduct an investigation like a D.A. would on rackets—under cover."

Louie looked up at the words "D.A.."

"We need evidence," Rogers continued. "When we get enough, we'll drag Sontag into court. Put a stop injunction on every magazine he's got. But you can't waste a single hour. His bookkeeper works at night. Go up there. Get in. You'd never get past the front door in daylight. Start from that angle. Bribe any guy if you have to. You know the ropes Johnny."

"Sure," Johnny said.

Rogers rose. "Time is the essence. Either Sontag breaks me—or I break him!" He shouldered into his coat. "There's one other thing. At midnight Dulcy Dickens arrives in Grand Central Station. I want you to——"

"Dulcy Dickens!" Moe said.

Rogers smiled, dropped on the desk an envelope containing three copies of a contract. "I want her signed up to my company. You'll find the contracts fair—with a rising word rate scale—up to four cents a word. But be sure you get her to sign *tonight!*"

"Otherwise Sontag——"

"That's right. He'll get her. Put Miss Dickens in a good hotel. Buy her a midnight supper. Treat her right." Joe Rogers adjusted his scarf, put on his hat.

"Mr. Rogers," Moe said, "she hasn't got an agent, has she?"

"Why no, she hasn't."

"Do you think—by any chance—that I could——"

"I don't see why not," Joe said. "Just write an agent's rider into the contracts. I'm sure it'll be agreeable with her."

At the very thought of a client like Dulcy Dickens Moe had paled. He slipped off the table.

"You're a very fine man, Mr. Rogers," he said. "You are a friend in need. I will long remember——"

But Joe Rogers had gone. Johnny followed him into the hall.

When Johnny returned he was fingering a fifty dollar bill. Moe stared at it.

"Part of the retainer fee," Johnny said. "He's going to send a check for the rest." He sat down in the swivel chair and parked his feet on the desk. "Moe," he said, "we're in." He glanced at Louie. "Kid, you can come with us tonight—to meet the hottest pulp writer since the great and immortal Horatio Alger."

"And I'm going to be her agent," Moe breathed. He was a little dazed.

"Not me," Louie said. "I can't come with you. I got to be at a meeting with some citizens in town to see about getting Les out on bail."

"My God," Johnny said, "they aren't going to let him *out*, are they?"

"If they don't—he's going to break out."

"From the Tombs? Don't make me laugh!"

"You'll see," Louie said naively.

Johnny sighed and wrapped the fifty dollar bill around one finger. It seemed very good to be working again. Like old times. He wondered now why he'd ever stopped being a detective. He had no more love for Sontag than Rogers did, and he was fairly sure he could work up some kind of a case.

A few minutes before ten that night he slipped into the Mauser Building, and beat it up the back stairs. He wore a trenchcoat, tied with a belt. A felt hat, wet from snow, was shoved back on his head. In one of his pockets he carried a flashlight. He climbed the eight flights of stairs to the floor rented by Sontag Publications. In the main editorial room, lights were on and scrub women worked, mopping up.

Johnny sauntered in casually, as though he were one of the employees. He walked over to a desk. He opened the drawer and made a motion of rummaging through it. He saw a battered manuscript from an author in Delaware—an editorial veto on it in large letters *NO*. Johnny erased this and wrote *YES—terrific—buy at once!*

"You're welcome," he said to the manuscript.

He moved away from the desk now and looked around for the bookkeeper's office. Eventually, he found the englassed cubicle. It was dark and empty. Johnny turned to one of the scrub women.

"Isn't what's-his-name around tonight?" It had occurred to him that Rogers was probably right—a Sontag accountant would be underpaid and he could lead up to the point where he could make a deal. At least a try in that direction would be a start.

"You mean Mr. Clark?" the woman asked. "He comes in sometimes—but I ain't seen him tonight."

Johnny walked down a short corridor. There was a light in Sontag's private office, and through the frosted glass door he saw both Sontag's silhouette and that of a girl. Voices hummed faintly over the transom, but he couldn't make out what they were saying. For a moment he stood and admired the sharp curves of the girl's shadow. Then he started back.

He wandered forlornly across the scrubbed floors in the big editorial room and started for the stairs. But the elevator door stood open, and the operator was talking to the night watchman. The watchman looked up and Johnny stepped innocently into the elevator. When the door at last closed, and the operator turned, Johnny saw his face for the first time.

"Mike Curtis—what the hell!"

The dungaree-clad man grinned. He'd known Johnny

back in the days of the former detective agency. Mike Curtis had been running an elevator then, too.

"What are you doing here, Johnny?"

"Oh, I just dropped in," Johnny said. "Wanted to see my old pal, Sontag."

"Yeah? You're a big writer now, aren't you?"

"Well—I was," Johnny said. He was anxious to disarm the man. "Drop in on me sometimes, Mike. We'll have a drink and talk over old times."

"Swell," Curtis said.

The elevator stopped at the ground floor, and the door opened. Johnny started out. But Mike suddenly called:

"Where you staying now?"

"Oh, at the—" he caught himself. "At the Palace Towers," he said, on inspiration. "You know, Fifty-ninth Street."

"Gee, real class, huh?"

"Nothing but the best," Johnny said.

Outside, he started up the street. The gutters were black with slush, and taxis swished by. There were overcoated men, and girls in galoshes; the lights of the city shone yellow through a flurry of white. Johnny looked up at the electric clock. It was twenty minutes to eleven. He turned in at a bar, opened his coat, and put his foot on the rail.

"Whiskey straight," he said. "Soda on the side."

It was the first time in weeks that he'd been able to spend money like this, and he felt good. The bar was crowded, and a radio played low. Johnny had time to kill until midnight. He reached one hand into his trenchcoat pocket for cigarettes. The package was wet with snow, and he brushed it off. What a helluva sweet title, he thought: *Snow in My Pocket.* He downed the drink, ordered another, and turned the title this way and that in his mind. It was good for a novel at least.

At twenty-five minutes past eleven, when the scrub women had left, the night watchman knocked gently on the door of Sam Sontag's private office. A light still glowed brightly inside the watchman wished to inquire how long it would be needed. When there was no answer to his knock he tried again a little harder this time. There was only silence and, here alone in the dark corridor, the watchman was somewhat alarmed. He turned his hand on the knob and opened the office door. Then he stared.

Sam Sontag lay face up. His skin was like wax, and the watchman could see the white down of his side-burns. Sontag's eyes were wide open, and a knife, stuck in his chest, stood straight up. It was a hunting knife and the leather sheath was on the floor beside the body.

Snow was falling gently past the window.

CHAPTER FIVE

IT WAS JUST after midnight, and in Grand Central Station, on the upper level, Redcaps hurried through Gate 14, going down the long catwalk to the train platform. A red sign glowed brightly above the gate marked *Southern Limited.* People were gathering, waiting to meet the passengers when they came up. Johnny arrived breathlessly, Moe on his heels. Johnny stood on tiptoes looking over the heads of the crowd. Somebody said in a loud voice that the train was just now pulling in. Moe's round, sad face flushed. He wore a shabby tweed coat, a gray scarf, and a black derby. He pulled woolen mittens deeper over his fingers.

"We're almost late," he said. "I knew I shouldn't have stopped for that buttermilk."

"Take it easy, Uncle," said Johnny, "we've got time to throw away."

But even as he spoke, passengers began coming through the gate, followed by Redcaps loaded down with luggage. Someone rushed up and flung her arms around a bespeckled old woman. "Aunt Sesame! How are you, darling!" Other passengers were coming through steadily now.

"How in the hell are we going to recognize her?" Moe said.

"We can't miss," Johnny said, keeping his eyes peeled. "Rogers gave me an old snapshot of her. Besides, female writers are all the same. Tailored clothes, stringy hair. A portable in one hand; a mangey suitcase in the other. They're always——"

His voice choked off. A small, radiantly beautiful girl flounced through the gate, carrying in her arms a shaggy white poodle. She was followed by two Redcaps, each bearing luggage.

"Look," Moe said, "a safari!"

Johnny only stared. The girl was about twenty-two, her cheeks dimpled, her face emotion itself—saucy, naughty, gay, sad—as though she had stepped out of a water color from Paris. Her jet-black hair was crazily windblown, with audacious bangs; her eyes were green, slanted, kitten eyes. She wore a light tan coat, thrown back off her shoulders, tan galoshes and beret, the beret pulled over on one side of her head. Her breasts were straight and sharp against a soft, woolly sweater, and her hips, swinging gracefully as she walked, enhanced a neat, tight skirt. Her stockings were sheer silk.

"She's like a dream I used to have," Johnny said.

"It—it *could* be Dulcy," Moe suggested.

"So could I, Uncle. But I ain't."

"You could ask her, couldn't you?"

"Well, I——" Johnny suddenly chased after her. He tapped her shoulder. "Pardon me, are you——"

She turned and faced him. Her dark black eyes sparkled. Her lips were burning red. Johnny lost his voice, gestured foolishly with his hands. The fluffy white poodle regarded him with button eyes.

"I—I work for a radio quiz show," Johnny said. "We're—collecting girls named Dulcy Dickens. Of course that isn't your name, and I——"

"Ah, but it *is* my name," she said.

"It—is—your—name," Johnny repeated. "Well, I'm sorry to have bothered you, I—*what did you say?*"

She laughed.

They were in a cafe on the upper level, sipping coffee. Dulcy Dickens' feet were hooked on the lower rung of the stool, and the poodle was looking forlornly up at them. Dulcy sipped her coffee, green eyes coquettish and she glanced rapidly from one to the other.

"Are you sure you won't have a hamburger?" Moe asked. "Mr. Rogers said we should give you a midnight supper."

"No, this is fine," she said.

"There's a—a—matter of a contract," Moe said, fishing inside his coat. "Have you a pen?"

"Oh, that can wait," Dulcy said.

"Sure," Johnny agreed. "Until we get to the hotel," he added.

"We are going to a hotel?"

"The best in town," Johnny said. "Moe and I are going to install you. In fact, now that——"

"Now that times are better," Moe said.

"Yes, now that prosperity is here, we are thinking of taking a suite in the same hotel."

"Just for a few days," Moe said, "to see that you meet all the right people."

"Such as Mr. Rogers," said Johnny.

"You are both very kind! What is the name of this hotel?"

"Why, the—the——" Johnny paused. "The Palace Towers," he said, finally.

Moe's face sagged. "But——"

"Fifteen dollars a day," Johnny said. "Just until you get—located."

"Ah, but who is going to pay for this?"

"Yes," Moe said, "tell us."

"Why you two embarrass me," Johnny said. "Mr. Rogers will pay. Dulcy—from the contract. Myself—from the work I am doing for him." He gazed at Dulcy. "Those historic romances you do are terrific."

"Do you——" Moe crossed his fingers—"write very fast?"

"No," she said. "About four stories a week is all I do. Of course, I realize that isn't very much, but——"

Johnny choked on his coffee.

Moe cleared his throat. "We won't press you. But do five a week if you can."

She nodded gravely. "I will try."

"How'd you get started in this racket?" Johnny asked.

"Somebody gave to me a writer's magazine, and I read articles about the—what they call—the pulps." Her voice was low, soft. "Naturally, I have never tried the big magazines. I know my stories are not good enough. Perhaps maybe later, you think?"

"I don't even want to try to think," Johnny said.

"My great-grandfather was a writer," Dulcy went on. She laughed. "Poor fellow. He wrote much faster than I. Tons of stories. Mama said perhaps maybe it runs in the family."

"Perhaps maybe she's right," said Johnny. "You're French, aren't you?"

"Yes." She whisked back the bangs. "Mama and I have an apartment in New Orleans. Papa owned a curio store in the quarter. He is dead now, and Mama tries to run it best she can, but she really knows very little about the business." She dropped the poodle a crumb of hamburger from Moe's plate. "You eat that, Kiki. It will make you a fat little dog."

She looked up, wiping her hands on a napkin. Her fingernails were polished a glistening red.

"Poor Mama!" she sighed reflecting. "Papa used to say some of his antiques were worth a fortune. But Mama has been able to extract only the most wretched prices. The silver candlesticks that belonged to Napoleon—do you know what we got?—a hundred dollars, no more! So now that I am in New York, I must send Mama money."

"I always imagined that Dickens was an English name," Johnny said.

"Oh, but yes, it is!" Dulcy said. "I use it only for my writing."

"A nom-de-plume?"

"*Oui.* How pretty you say that, Shonny! Soon, perhaps, I shall tell you what is my real name." She glanced up. "But not now. Not until I am ready to write real stories."

"Okay," Johnny said. He paid the check. "Shall we go to the hotel?"

"Yes," Dulcy said. "I am anxious to unpack. I have brought with me some fine new lingerie. I have two trunks that arrive tomorrow by express."

Moe stepped back off the stool. "That's funny," he said, "I didn't know there was a rug——" The poodle began to yip bloody murder.

Johnny said: "Get off the dog, you lug!"

Dulcy snatched Kiki up in her arms. The whimpering poodle gave Moe a dirty look. Moe tipped his hat. "I'm sorry, doggie." He reached out his hand. Kiki snapped at it.

"Look," Johnny said, "you just get the bags, and don't worry about it."

He swung off with Dulcy. Moe's eyes followed them, then he pulled his derby down on his head, and started picking up the luggage, piece by piece.

Dulcy Dickens marched into the lavish hotel suite,

Kiki, the poodle, under one arm. Johnny and Moe followed, and behind them came the bellboys carrying the baggage. They set it down; Moe gave them a dime each, and they departed. "Swell hotel," he said. "Did you see the way they lingered at the door? They wanted to be sure everything was all right." Johnny had registered for himself and Moe in a suite across the hall. Dulcy walked around the room, inspecting the chintz curtains, imitation fireplace, built-in radio. The windows overlooked Central Park, bony trees etched in charcoal against the white snow that covered the ground. Street traffic swished by far below.

Dulcy laughed happily. "I am so excited. We do not see snow in New Orleans. I am going to like New York. Where is it I sleep?"

Johnny nodded toward a door.

"Ah, another room! But this is too much!"

"You'll get used to it," Johnny said.

"There's the little matter of a contract," Moe said, "I——"

"You think so, Shonny? You think I will get used to it? I am a poor girl only."

"Cinderella."

"About these contracts," Moe said.

"Really, Shonny? You think I am like her?"

She stood fresh and lovely against the backdrop of Manhattan winter. She put the poodle down, whisked back her windblown bangs. Watching her, Johnny did not know why, but he was enchanted. He remembered himself, five years ago, how eager he'd been. Suddenly he didn't want her to be hurt.

"Little French Cinderella," he said, "and New York in the winter."

"Shonny, you're poetic!"

"Whacky's the word," he said. "I'm that way sometimes."

"Now, these contracts," Moe said.

"I like you that way."

"The contract says——"

"We'll get along," Johnny said.

Moe slammed the contracts to the floor. The poodle

jumped, then began to bark at him. Moe backed up, the poodle following, barking furiously.

"Will you—please God—get this animal——"

There was a knock at the door. Johnny opened it. Two plainclothesmen stepped into the room. They glanced around. Dulcy was rescuing Moe from the poodle.

One of the detectives turned to Johnny.

"That balk-headed guy—that John Saxon?"

"I'm Saxon," Johnny said.

There was a click and he was deftly handcuffed to one of the men. Johnny's head came up.

"What the hell is——"

"A guy named Sontag's been murdered," the detective said. "People are saying you did it. We want you to come downtown."

"Yeah," said the other. "One of the D.A.'s men is getting up a surprise party."

"Sontag murdered! But I——"

They hauled him into the corridor. Flashlight cameras exploded. Reporters fell in step behind Johnny.

"What about it, Saxon? Got anything to say?"

"I did it with a hatchet," Johnny said. He was struggling, looking back over his shoulder. Dulcy arrived at the door, her expression one of horror.

"Listen, kid," Johnny yelled. "I'll be right back. I—"

She nodded, perplexed. "*Bientot*, Shonny!"

CHAPTER SIX

THE WALLS of the room were green, and the lights were hot and bright. Outside, trucks slushed by on Centre Street, and now and then there was the dying siren of a patrol car pulling in at headquarters. Johnny sat at a nicked and cigarette-burned walnut table, leaning on his elbows. He licked his parched lips. Three detectives had grilled him for an hour, but now they had vanished. They would be replaced by a new police contingent. For the moment the room was empty. Johnny glanced at the barred window, searched again through his pockets for a cigarette. They'd taken his cigarettes, wallet, belt and tie.

The door opened and D. A. Small walked in. Johnny recognized him—the bespeckled mouse who stood on the fringe of all official City Hall group pictures. He was one of the assistants in the D. A.'s office—plump, sleek, well-fed. He wore a pince-nez which hung on a black ribbon. He was followed by police captain, Nick Willis—bushy white hair, beet-red face, a foot taller than his compànion. Two uniformed cops and a clerk came in behind the officials. Everyone was standing but Johnny.

"Well, now," Small said, standing legs astride, fingering the pince-nez. "What have we here?" He had the pleasant, patronizing air of a Y.M.C.A. life member.

"We have a citizen accused of murder," Johnny said.

"Why don't you confess, Saxon,"Willis said. His voice was deep, booming. "Make it easier all round?"

"I daresay it would," Johnny ventured.

Willis turned to the D. A.'s man. "Saxon used to be a detective, Mr. Small. He isn't like our other prisoners. He knows the procedure, don't you, Saxon?"

"You're putting me to sleep," Johnny said.

Small's tinny voice lashed out. "You know you killed Sontag! Why don't you admit it?"

"I just can't seem to get in the mood," Johnny replied.

"Let's go over the circumstances," Small said. "At some time around ten o'clock you were seen in Sam Sontag's publishing office. Two of the cleaning women were in here a few minutes ago and identified you. At ten-thirty you left the Mauser Building, riding down to the main floor on the freight elevator. You talked with Mike Curtis, the operator, and told where you were living."

"That's where I slipped up," Johnny said. "I see it all now!"

Small threw up his hands.

"He's a tough monkey," Willis said. "Let me work on him."

"Sure," Johnny said. "Take off my shoes and burn the soles of my feet with matches. That ought to do it."

The Assisstant D. A. resumed. "*Why* did you go to see Sontag at that time of night?"

"I'll tell you," Johnny said. "He wouldn't see me in the daytime. I wanted to talk to him about a story. I used to do pretty good ones. In fact, they were damn good!"

"Ah, he wouldn't see you in the daytime. Avoided you whenever he could. You were broke, desperate . . . bided your time, waited until you knew he was working late . . . burst into his office. An argument ensued. You flew into a rage. You'd been brooding, sulking for days. You picked up the sheathed hunting knife he used for a paper weight—unsheathed it—there was a scuffle. You plunged the knife into his chest!"

"Rejection," Johnny quoted, "does not necessarily imply lack of merit."

"What do you mean?" the attorney squeaked, his face livid.

"Poor motivation," Johnny said.

"You think so? You think for one minute our D. A. couldn't make a jury of twelve believe that? You are mistaken! A famous publisher—a starving, embittered writer——"

"Did that forty bucks you found in my wallet look like starvation?"

"I——"

"It shoots your pretty story full of holes," Johnny said.

"You might have stolen it! You just admitted you wanted to see him about doing a story, making money."

"Yes—but I discovered he was busy. And I got cold feet, never went into his office."

"In what way was he busy?" Willis asked.

"He had company, a girl. Probably his secretary. No doubt you've already checked on that."

One of the uniformed cops, engrossed in the proceedings, nodded.

"You stay out of it!" Small screamed at him.

"Since the girl left *after* I did," Johnny said, "and must have taken the same freight elevator down—that alibis me right out of the picture. Sontag was alive when she left him or I presume as much."

Small looked at his watch. "How do we know that once you left the Mauser Building you didn't return by way of the back stairs—the way you sneaked in to begin with? How do we know the girl didn't scare you away the first time—so that you decided to wait until after she left the building—until you could be sure Sontag was alone? How do we know that *then* you didn't go up and kill him?"

"How *do* you know?" Johnny said.

Small blew up. "This man is impossible, Captain Willis!"

"Have you an alibi for after you left the building that first time?" Willis asked.

"Yeah, I went to a bar just down the street," Johnny said. "I tipped the bartender two-bits, and he said tips weren't necessary and didn't want to take it—so he'll remember me."

White-haired Nick Willis glanced at the attorney.

Small placed the pince-nez in his vest pocket. "There's very little more we can get out of him tonight," he said. "But I will not tolerate his insolence! I want him held." His tiny round eyes came up. "As a material witness."

Johnny leaped from his chair. "You can't do that!"

"Sit down," Willis said.

Small turned and walked from the room. Willis looked at the cops, and nodded toward Johnny. "Lock him up. You heard what peanuts said."

"A stinking trick!" Johnny said.

"I know," Willis replied. "But what can I do? Peanuts was hollering because the boys didn't break you down. He was going to do it. They want everything on a platter in this place. Just dip up some bail, Saxon, and I'll get a judge to set it tonight if you want."

"But I haven't got a dime!" Johnny said.

"Then you're up a creek, aren't you?"

"I'm——"

Johnny never finished. Nick Willis had left.

The cell in the Tombs was cold and wet, and an icy wind blew in through the barred window. Johnny paced up and down, smoking a cigarette. They'd returned his pack—but not his tie or belt. A prisoner sleeping in an upper bunk woke and sat propped on his elbow for a full three minutes, watching Johnny, his eyes moving up and down as Johnny walked. At last he lay down and went back to sleep. He began to snore.

At four in the morning there were footsteps in the corridor. Johnny was sitting on his bunk now and he looked up. A flashlight was turned on him, the cell door opened. Johnny slipped on his shoes, stood up without lacing them. He stepped into the corridor beside the motioning jailer. The two of them moved toward the lighted office at the end of the cell block. There was a small, withered lawyer here—his face wrinkled, red and mischievous, like a monkey's—leaning over a varnished table hastily signing papers. A police sergeant, and a lieutenant stood by, looking sleepy. The lawyer straightened up, stared at Johnny with bright little eyes.

"Hello," he said. He put out his hand. "I'm Steinmetz."

Johnny rubbed his eyes against the sudden bright light.

"We're getting you out," Steinmetz said. "They asked only a thousand dollars bail. I paid it in cash."

"But where did you——"

"Get the money? You have friends, my boy. Good, dear friends who would not see you languish behind bars." Steinmetz looked up and spoke for all to hear. "Mr. Saxon is a detective." He nodded wisely. "If it turns out that he's the one to solve the Sontag murder, it will not at all surprise me."

"It will me," Johnny said. Who in the hell had laid out a grand—in cash—for his bail?

He signed a few papers, then put his foot up on a chair and laced his shoes. Steinmetz packed his brief-case, tucked it under his arm, and was off down a lighted corridor. At this hour in the morning his footsteps echoed hollowly. Johnny slipped into his trenchcoat, slapped his hat on, collected his wallet, tie and belt—jamming the stuff in his pocket, he walked out the street door.

Outside, it had stopped snowing, but there was a cold, gray chill in the early morning darkness. Johnny turned up his collar and started down the stone steps. But he stopped halfway. He looked to his left. A heavy-set man in a dark coat stood at his side. He glanced right. A smaller, but harder, man was on his other side. He was flanked.

"Let's all go somewhere for breakfast," Johnny said.

"*Shuddup!*"

Johnny shut up.

"All right, you wise punk. Down the steps and across the curb. That's the baby. Climb into the back of that sedan and keep your trap closed."

Johnny crossed the sidewalk and got into a car. Outside the car door he saw the legs of the smaller man—crisp, tailored trousers, black shoes with built-up heels. He thought he had smelled jasmine. The man swung open the door and climbed in now. The other was behind the wheel, shifting gears. The Packard sedan began to roll. The tires sucked through the slush, throwing up a sheet of muddy water.

"I'm Jasper Ward."

"I've heard of you," Johnny said.

Ward fell silent. He flicked a lighter, lit a cigarette. He wore a dark blue shirt, an orange tie; his top coat was thrown open and Johnny could see an orange 'kerchief in his breast pocket. His face was calm, his eyes a light gray. It was the eyes, the dilated pupils, the smooth, cold pallor of his carefully massaged and talcumed face, that chilled Johnny.

"I paid your bill," Ward said. He put the lighter back in his pocket. "I got my personal lawyer out of bed. He had to call a judge to set the bail. You were a lot of trouble!"

"I probably don't deserve a word of it," Johnny said.

"Don't flip with me! You'll deserve it all right, and if you don't——" Ward puffed at the cigarette. "I don't waste my money. Or my time. I'm a business man!"

"I can see you're all business," Johnny said.

Ward reached over to slap Johnny's face. Johnny grabbed his wrist, and in almost the same moment there was a gun in Ward's other hand.

"Drive up an empty street and stop, Eli!"

The sedan wheeled hard left. Johnny released Ward's wrist, watched him, watched the gun. The car pulled up, the tires scraping a high curb. Eli turned off the lights, sat mutely behind the wheel. Johnny saw the big man's eyes watching him from the rear view mirror. Ward sat in the back seat. Johnny was cold as ice. Somewhere a church bell began to chime. There was a bead of sweat on Johnny's frozen cheek. Ash cans were rattling far down the street. Ward held the gun in deft, delicate fingers . . . waited. At last he spoke:

"You want it?"

Johnny didn't answer. He wasn't sure that he could.

"You've got one more chance," Ward said. "I don't want any more of your crap. People don't fool with me. Not for long, anyway."

"What is it you want?"

"That's better," Ward said. "You talk to me like that all the time. What I want is Dulcy Dickens. I want to know where she is."

"Why——"

"Don't lie to me! I warn you!" He looked up. "Drive, Eli." To Johnny: "I know you met her at the train. You and the cue-ball agent. And I want her. Fast. Before she signs any contracts. You've got her hid somewhere. And I——"

"I've got her hid?" The car had started again.

"You heard me! Did Joe Rogers think he was pulling anything on me? I know every move he makes. It'll be a sweet day in June before he beats me out of anything! Where is she?"

"Dulcy?"

"Quit stalling!"

"I—I can find her for you in the morning," Johnny said. His fingers were crossed. Obviously, Ward hadn't been to the Palace Towers. He knew of the meeting in Grand Central, but not of where they had taken Dulcy afterward.

The sedan was speeding down Seventh Avenue, swerving out around milk trucks, running red lights. Ward put away his gun.

"What do you mean—in the morning? This is morning!"

"I've got to wait until offices open," Johnny said. "So I can phone people. I don't know where she is right now. Hell, I've been in jail all night. But I'll find out for you, see? Say, I phone you at ten o'clock. I'll have news by then."

"You'll have more than that. You'll have her . . . and if you don't——"

"Yeah," Johnny said, "I catch."

"And if you do have her, and get me that contract," Ward said, "there's a bonus in it for you—a cool grand."

"A thousand bucks! But——" Johnny stared through the darkness at Ward. "Is it that important?"

"What do you think?"

"Well, I——"

"No. I take that back. Don't try to think. Just produce. Where'll I let you off?"

"Bellvedere Hotel," Johnny said.

Ward looked at him curiously.

When they pulled up in front of the Bellvedere, Johnny got out. He watched as the sedan drove off, then turned and pushed through the revolving door into the lobby. He found a bellboy, slipped a dollar into his palm, and told him to take him out the service exit. The uniformed boy led the way. On the street again, Johnny's anxious eyes searched for sign of the Packard sedan. He didn't see it. He walked quickly to a hack stand, climbed into a cab—and again making sure he hadn't been followed—told the driver:

"Palace Towers."

At the Palace Towers he looked up and down Fifty-ninth Street. The sky was gray with dawn, and the snow in the park looked very white. Seeing no one, Johnny ducked into the hotel. His wet, worn shoes sunk into the thick rug. A mahogany panelled elevator shot him up to the thirtieth floor. He discovered that he still had in his pocket the keys to Dulcy's apartment and the keys to his and Moe's suite. He unlocked the door of his, opened it, and walked in.

"Moe!"

Moe sat in a chair, holding an ice pack on his face. His lips were cracked. Both his eyes were black and swollen. Skin has been torn off the tip of his left cheek. He looked up.

"Johnny—how'ja get—*ouch!*—outa the can?"

Johnny only stared at him. "What the hell hit you?"

"A cub—couple guys were here earlier," Moe explained, with effort. "They were looking for Dulcy."

"But I thought——"

"What?"

"Good Lord! I thought they didn't know about the Palace Towers. I didn't think they knew she was here!"

"They—knew all right," Moe said. "A guy named Eli did this——" he fanned his hands toward his face. "Kep—kept asking where is Dulcy. I said, I don't know—and he holds me up against the wall—every time I say I don't know—*bang!* And somebody in an orange shirt stands around and tells him how to do it!"

Johnny felt foolish that he'd taken so many precautions getting here from the Bellvedere, but he looked warmly at his old friend. "You mean you stood there—took that, lied to them—and all the time you knew she was in the suite just across the hall. Moe, sometimes I think——"

"Wait a minute," Moe said. "She ain't across the hall." He nursed his bruised lip. "Earlier tonight I we-went down to Centre Street to see if I could help you. When I got back she was gone!"

"What're you talking about?"

"I swear it!"

Johnny opened the door and walked across the corridor. He knocked, then used the key and went in. Dulcy's bags stood near the chintz curtains. Johnny strode into the bedroom. He looked into closets, out on the terrace, in the bathroom, the kitchenette, behind the divan. When he finished, Moe was standing there.

"I tell you she's walked out!"

"But she didn't know anybody in town and—hell, Moe, this is serious!"

"Yeah. That's what Eli said every time he smacked me."

CHAPTER SEVEN

THREE HOURS later, at nine that Saturday morning, Johnny stepped out of a steaming hot shower and groped for a towel. When he had found one, rubbed briskly his long legs and wet ears, he discovered that laid out for him in the dressing room was a brand-new striped robe, expensive form-fitting shorts—the kind you see in the ads—a ribbed silk under shirt, new socks, and handkerchiefs, wrapped the robe around himself, pushed his silk-stockinged feet into new red leather slippers, and strode into the living-room. Moe was here arranging a silver coffee set, toast with the crusts cut off, eggs, cereal and cream. He looked up brightly.

"Wait a minute," Johnny said. "Don't say a word." He fingered the robe, undershirt. "Where did we get these—shall I call them elegant?—things?"

"The haberdasher downstairs," Moe reported. "It will be on the bill." Moe himself was wearing a red silk robe and blue pajamas imported from Paris.

"And the breakfast?"

"Room Service," said Moe. "It came to only two dollars. I signed the check."

"I see. I don't want to upset you—but what are we going to use for dough?"

"The fee you soak Joe Rogers." Moe said. "As a detective—if not as a writer—you come high."

"It's pleasant to know that. Let's see, we were employed to investigate Mr. Sam Sontag. I didn't tell the police that, because I always protect a client—short of going to the electric chair for him. But, do you begin to see——"

"My God," said Moe, "do you think——"

"You can't very well investigate the business of a dead man. And up until the hour he died, we accomplished nothing to warrant any size fee. In fact, we owe Joe Rogers fifty bucks."

"But—but what are we going to do, Johnny?"

Johnny sat down in front of the breakfast tray. "We can't do anything.We didn't come in with any luggage so if we move out, according to law, it's conspiracy to defraud an innkeeper; the extras you've charged makes it larceny."

"Honest to God?"

"I wouldn't kid you, Uncle," Johnny said. "The only thing we can do is stay here until we get money. From somewhere. I'll have the bill put on a monthly basis. In a big place like this you can do that—even for food and other incidentals. So that gives us thirty days."

"Then?"

Johnny smiled grimly, and drew his finger across his throat. Moe gulped, and pushed his breakfast away from him. Johnny on the other hand, began to eat. He had not slept, but the shower had refreshed him. Outside, the sky was the color of slate—'Gray Saturday'—it wasn't even a good title, he thought. His head ached just a little, and he sipped at the coffee.

Suddenly, he was remembering Dulcy's laughter . . . the perfume she used, the way she'd whisk back her wind-blown hair; how she said, "I like you that way, Shonny." He did not know why he should remember this, only that he did, and in a way that hurt him—like a sad little melody could sometimes hurt him. She was gone. He'd canvassed the bellboys, all the clerks; no one had seen her go out. He'd searched for a clue, any sane reason for her disappearance, and had found none. Glamour in the pulps, he thought. She had too much of it. She should have stayed in New Orleans. He set the coffee cup down.

"What's eating *you?*" Moe said.

"Nothing why?"

"You look like *The Motif Tragic.*"

"I was thinking of Dulcy."

"Yeah," Moe said. "As long as she was going to vanish, she might have had the decency to sign those contracts."

"Shut up!"

"Hey, what *is* wrong?"

"It's just that—well, everything's lousy," Johnny said. He rubbed his hand down over his face. He wished that he could be more analytical about it and less emotional. "That poodle's a clue, of course . . ."

"Clue, hell, it's a menace!" Moe leaned forward. "Do you think, by any chance, Dulcy's disappearance is tied in with Sontag's murder? She was his writer originally, you know."

Johnny's eyes came up. "You've got it! Find Dulcy, and——"

"And we've got the killer! Take the case yourself, Johnny. You won't get any pay, maybe, or any thanks, but—oh, boy! Swell publicity! It's just what *I Never Sleep* needs."

Johnny looked at him with disgust.

"You were a swell cop," Moe said. "You always were. You can work for nothing this once. The hotel'll understand."

"Oh—sure!"

Moe snapped his fingers. "Maybe Room Service would even pay your expense account!"

"Why, certainly!"

"I'll call downstairs and ask them," Moe said. "Think of the boon to the Palace Towers." He reached for the phone.

"Put that down, stupid!"

"But, Johnny——"

"If they so much as suspected I was anything as common as a detective they'd use us for defamation of the hotel's character."

"What about me?" Moe asked. "A literary agent."

"Shh," Johnny said. "Not so loud. Don't you know what they'd do to a pulp agent?"

"What?"

Johnny shuddered. "Let's not even discuss it. But as for Dulcy. I won't be working for nothing. There are a number of people who probably want to see her." He glanced at his fingernails. "You can't tell. I may be one of them."

"Johnny, you ain't getting sentimental?" Moe seemed worried.

"It's been a long time since the last time I was in love," Johnny said. He reflected. "That'd make a good song title, wouldn't it? Only it's too long." He reached for the phone. "Get me Bellevue Hospital," he told the operator. "Missing Persons Bureau. It's the office next door to the morgue." He held the phone in his lap and waited.

"Maybe—maybe Dulcy's dead," Moe said.

Johnny's eyes went cold.

"Maybe she's been kidnapped," Moe went on. "Beautiful little French girl——"

"And just maybe," Johnny interrupted, "we're going to turn Manhattan inside out and find her!" He picked up the receiver of the phone again. A voice had come through on the wire. "I want to report a missing person," Johnny said. "The name is . . ."

DULCY DICKENS, WRITER, MISSING; MAY BE CLUE IN SONTAG MURDER

Death of Publisher Unsolved as G-Men Join Police in Widespread Search for New Orleans Writer

Johnny put down the tabloid, and looked up. He was sitting on a corner of Sontag's desk, in the office where the body had been found. It was now a quarter to eleven.

"It's just off the press," Kay Leigh said. "A messenger rushed it over."

In the room besides the slim, dark-haired secretary, was Police Captain Nick Willis. He looked sleepy and harassed. Kay Leigh wore a tight-fitting yellow dress that contrasted the beauty of her olive skin, and her dark eyes.

"I didn't know the company worked on Saturday," Johnny said.

"We don't usually," Kay explained. She looked him over, a little hungrily, tapping a pencil against her orange-red lips. "But we're getting out two new magazines," she went on. "Mr. Sontag instructed everybody to come to work today."

"He—what?"

"That was before he died."

"Oh."

"What'd you think?" Willis said. "He sent a message from his slab in the morgue?"

"Today," Kay continued, "Mr. Ward phoned and

said that all of our schedules were to be carried out as usual—or even a little faster and more efficiently. He said Mr. Sontag would have wanted it that way."

"How touching!" Johnny said. "But what the hell has Ward got to do with it, anyway?"

"That's an interesting angle," Willis interjected. "In the contract between Sontag and Ward there's a clause that states that in the event of the death of one, the other inherits the business."

Johnny lifted his eyebrows.

"It's my idea," Willis said, "that Sontag was Ward's puppet, and all he has to do now is appoint another. It's ethics—and in some states the law—for a distributor to be actively engaged as a publisher. In order to cover up the fact that he was promoting the Sontag chain, Ward also distributes various minor publications—church journals, and stuff like that—from other companies."

Johnny looked at him. "How'd you get so bright, Cap?"

Willis shrugged. "It's nothing, old man," he said sarcastically. "I know how you writers feel about city cops. But once in a while we assemble a few facts—just so the taxpayers won't become too annoyed with the graft we take in."

Johnny winced. He'd written as many 'crooked cop' stories as the next. He made a mental note that that trend was on the wane.

"Actually," Willis said, "I've had undercover men working on the business angles up here since last night. We got 'Chick' Clark, the bookkeeper, out of bed. And a few others. The information I've just related, however, is the sum total of our discoveries."

"Not a bad sum."

"Oh, thank you," Willis snapped bitterly. "In our modest way, we plod along. Frankly, I expect the solution of the murder to come out of the business aspect. All we've gained so far is a sound motive for Ward to have bumped Sontag off."

"And Ward's alibied?"

"Well, yes, in a James Cagney sort of way. That's not

saying he couldn't have paid an assassin to come up here and do it."

"Exactly!" Johnny said. "Listen, I've been in the business for years. I know nearly every editor and publisher in town. Possibly I can help you. You give me a police permit, and——"

"Give you what?" Willis said.

Johnny saw the look in the white-haired captain's face. "Forget it." Kay Leigh was still watching Johnny. Her liquid eyes made him want to squirm.

"You can bet your last dollar I'll forget it," Willis said. "What I was trying to find over here was a motive for you to have committed the murder. One sounder than we had last night. Why do you think I called you at the Palace Towers and had you meet me here? To ask your help! Don't make me laugh!"

"Ouch," Johnny said.

"I'm convinced you weren't telling the whole truth last night," Willis went on. "I'm like a lie detector that way. I've grilled so many men I can tell a phoney every time! So don't try anything, see? Don't try to pull the wool over my eyes."

"I wouldn't want to," Johnny said, "they're too pretty."

"That's right! Keep it up, Saxon, and I'll have you booked for murder so fast you won't know what happened."

"Neither'll the public when I go on trial," Johnny said. "You're tired, pappy. Why don't you go home and beat your wife? You'll feel better."

"Another thing—what'd you do with Dulcy Dickens?"

"I've got her hid in a box car," Johnny said.

Willis regarded him coldly. "I've information she's been murdered."

Johnny tensed. He slid off the edge of the desk. Willis watched him.

"That's what I wanted to know," he said. "I have no information of any kind about her. But I wanted to see the look on your face. Well, I've seen it!" He looked Johnny up and down. But he was so sleepy he was almost blind. He glanced at his wrist watch, then he turned and went out.

The door slammed.

Johnny looked at the closed door. Then he turned back to Kay Leigh. She was watching him with wide, avid eyes. Her breast rose and fell as she breathed.

"Turn on the radio," Johnny said, "and we'll dance."

"You fool!" She walked out.

Johnny looked down at his hands. He was trembling. It wasn't because of Kay. But Dulcy, and the word 'murder' carelessly used.

The phone rang. Absently, he picked up the receiver.

"Hello," a voice said, "who is this?"

"This is me," said Johnny.

"Whoever you are, answer me, and answer me fast!"

"Oh, hello, Mr. Ward," Johnny said.

"Is that *you?*"

"If you mean me," Johnny said, "it is." He held the receiver away from his ear. The wire was burning.

CHAPTER EIGHT

OUTSIDE THE one window, across the court, a girl had entered a small room that faced the windows. The room was one of the many small cubicles of the type found in dress establishments. She was carrying a dress over her arm. She hung the dress over a chair and started pulling the one she was wearing over head. It got caught in her hair, and she stood with upstretched arms tugging at the dress. She was wearing panties and a brassiere, and she had a very fine figure. Her legs were long and smooth looking.

When Johnny listened again, Ward was saying, "Where is she? What about her? You were going to call me at ten o'clock."

"She's missing," Johnny said.

"That's hot! She's missing, eh? Maybe I read the papers, too. Ever think of that? Come again, you punk. Where's Dulcy?"

"I don't know."

The girl across the court finally managed to get her dress untangled from her head. Her hair was wavy and blonde.

"Do you remember what I said in the car this morning?"

"Perfectly."

"Do you think I was fooling?"

"No."

"Then where is she?"

"I don't know . . . this is where you came in."

"You said you could find her."

"I thought I could."

"There's only one thing that saves your life."

"What's that?" Johnny had an idea that the girl could see him from the window, but she made no attempt to pull down the shade.

"With all the cops in town looking for her," Ward said sharply, "it must be ligitimate."

"It is. She's as gone as Prohibition."

"Can you find her? From now on, I mean?"

"I'm going to try," Johnny said.

"Listen, you're a private cop, aren't you?"

"Well . . . I go through the motions."

"I'm raising the ante." The voice on the wire was smooth as silk. "If you find her, it's worth two grand to you."

"At least."

"What is this—a hold-up? Three grand, you thieving crook! And if this is a trick, you'll collect it in hell."

"Three grand's a deal, pappy," said Johnny.

"See that you find her! That's all . . ." There was a pause. Then, sharply, "Say what the hell are you doing in my office?"

"Nothing. Looking around, that's all." The girl had slipped into the new blue dress. She was smoothing it over her hips. She looked in a mirror, patted down her hair, and left the room. "Is it your office?" asked Johnny. "I thought it was Sontag's."

"You know damn well it's my office, you two-bit snooping punk. You stick your nose into my business affairs and it'll be the last you ever smell anything with it. How come you're up there anyway?"

Johnny frowned at the phone. "In the first place, I'm looking for Dulcy. Second, for Sontag's killer."

"Never mind Sontag!" What's it to you who killed him? And Dulcy isn't there. I don't want you anywhere near my place. Is that clear?"

"As clear as cyanide."

"All right, then, get the hell off my premises. There's going to be a lot of changes made up there. I'm branching out. And if you're hanging around you're going to be hurt in a way no hospital will be able to help. Do I make myself clear?"

"Which was better," Johnny asked, "this business or rum-running?"

The receiver almost exploded. Gently, Johnny hung it back on the hook.

Then, a few seconds later, he quietly removed it again and listened.

There was a humming sound disturbed by a slight click.

"Dammit to hell!" he said. He wondered if someone had been listening in on the line.

Johnny cradled the receiver and walked over to the window. The dressing room across the court was still deserted. He wondered if the girl had bought the blue dress, or would return to change into her old one. Overhead the sky was dull, cold gray, and shining through it like a vague coppery disk was the sun.

Behind him, Kay Leigh said quietly, "The view is better after dark, when the lights are on."

Johnny turned.

Kay stood slouched against the door. She had closed it behind her, quietly, and now her hands were behind her hips, resting on the knob. He started to say, "What——" and she nodded toward the dressing room windows across the court. Her dark eyes were inscrutable, but her implication was quite clear.

"Oh!" said Johnny, and then grinned. "They say you are never old until you stop looking."

Kay stood watching him, and the way she was standing with her hands behind her made her breasts push out against the sleekness of her tight-fitting yellow dress. Her breasts were firm and high and round. Her slim, tall body was seductiveness itself.

She finally spoke again. "You look tired." Her voice was slightly husky and low. "Like a drink?"

"What have you got?"

Kay smiled and came across the room. Her movements were unhurried and smooth, and he found himself watching her covertly. She had fine hips and long slim legs. She bent over and pulled out the bottom drawer of the desk. Turning her head, she asked, "Rye or Scotch?"

"Either one will help." He was tired. He had been hours without sleep, and he didn't know when he was going to get a chance to rest. There was something about Kay Leigh that made him forget this, though, when he looked at her.

She placed a bottle of Dewar's *Victoria Vat*—twelve

years old—on the desk and stepped across the office to a water cooler. She returned with three small paper cups, one filled with water. She put the cup with water on the desk, held the two empty ones while Johnny poured the drinks. He watched her as he filled her cup, and she nodded her head when the cup was almost half full. The pleasant bouquet of the whiskey mingled with Lentheric *Shanghai*, the perfume that was part of her disturbing seductiveness.

Kay held up her cup, "To Johnny Saxon, a fine writer." She took a sip of the whiskey. "Why did you ever quit, Johnny?" Her voice was warm.

He shrugged. "I was burned out, I guess." He tossed off the drink, took the water that she passed him. Her fingers brushed his hand. "Anyway, being a detective is more fun. You meet more people."

She finished her drink, and it left her sultry lips moist and orange-red. "No," she said, shaking her head. "You were good. I used to read a lot of your stories." Her slim hand was on his arm. "You were slated to go a long ways, Johnny Saxon. I know. You weren't burnt out you just needed a new stimulus."

"Such as?"

Her dark eyes were unreadable. "Perhaps I could help you."

She was standing close to him now, her tall, sleek body graceful and upsetting. The stiff shot of rye flowed through him and brought a warm glow to his body; it seeped into his brain and he felt very good indeed. She seemed to be aware of it also.

He grinned. "You sound like an agent. You sound like Moe."

"I didn't mean it that way, Johnny."

"How did you mean it?"

"I think——" she casually poured two more drinks, passing him one. "You need to be inspired by someone. Then you'll go places, Johnny." Her eyes left his own and searched the sensitive, lean lines of his face as she swallowed the drink. Then she met his gaze again.

"It's an idea," he said. And he thought, She's on the

make, all right, and she doesn't give a damn about making the fact known. "You'll have a good job here now," he continued after a moment. "With Sam Sontag gone——"

"I don't know about that. There's going to be a lot of changes."

"But——"

"And Jasper Ward doesn't like women."

That thought had not occurred to him until this moment. "Those kind usually don't," he agreed.

Her lips were very close to his face. They were tempting, scarlet ones. The second drink had started a pleasant buzz in his head. He held himself a little stiffly. "I guess it is going to be a little tough with Sam gone," he said.

She eyed him narrowly. "I don't go for old men, Johnny!"

"I didn't mean——"

The telephone rang. When she picked up the receiver, he could distinctively hear Jasper Ward's brittle voice say, "Listen, baby, is that goddam snooping Johnny Saxon still there?"

Kay had leaned across him in order to pick up the handset. Her whole body was quivering slightly as she talked calmly on the phone. She said quietly, "Well, he's around." And Johnny heard Ward snap. "Have Chick Clark give him a two-hundred dollar retainer, and then throw him the hell out of there!"

Johnny started to whisper, "Tell him to——" but Kay's slim fingers reached up and covered his mouth as she held the receiver away from her ear with the other hand. There was some more explosive crackling of the line, then Ward hung up. Kay replaced the receiver and smiled at him.

Her fingers slid from his mouth with a caressing gesture. "You see," she said, "I have already made you some money. I can do you a lot of good, besides inspiring you in your writing."

Her hands were on his shoulders now. She leaned forward and her downward curved lips were moist-crimson. His arm went around her waist and he kissed her. She clung to him fiercely.

Immediately he regretted this, because he found himself thinking of Dulcy Dickens. He couldn't explain why, but nevertheless he felt guilty. He thought of wind-blown hair, of unruly dark bangs, of that child's fresh eagerness. . .

He straightened and said abruptly, "Who the hell is Chick Clark?"

Kay said, "I'll call him."

CHAPTER NINE

KAY LEIGH led him along the inner office hallway, past the huge editorial room where a few of the editors were at work on various parts of the magazines. Mostly, though, they were standing around in small groups discussing the murder. Several looked up as Johnny and the girl passed the open doorway.

"Chick Clark is our bookkeeper," she was explaining. "He also signs the checks." Smiling as she indicated his mouth, she added, "You'd better wipe off that rouge."

Johnny used a clean pocket handkerchief which Moe Martin had bought for him that morning. He patted his lips as he followed Kay Leigh into the small, glass-enclosed room, in the corner of which was crowded a thin little man behind a huge desk.

"This is Johnny Saxon," Kay said. "I just spoke to you about him on the phone. Mr. Ward wants you to advance him two hundred dollars."

"For what!" Clark jumped to his feet and frowned at Johnny Saxon. His eyes looked like bright lemon drops behind thick-lensed glasses. His hair was thin, pale, and scraggly. "We don't give writers advances. You know that."

Johnny said, "I wouldn't write at your lousy rates if I was starving." He pulled out a pack of cigarettes, offered the girl one, and when she shook her head, lighted one for himself and hooked his leg over the edge of the desk. "Listen," he said to the bookkeeper, "get busy and write out that check."

"Mr. Saxon," explained Kay, "is trying to find Dulcy Dickens. The two-hundred dollars is some sort of retainer that Mr. Ward is paying him. I just talked to him on the phone."

"Talked to who?"

"Jasper Ward himself."

"And he said to pay it?"

"That's what I just told you," said Kay. She looked at Johnny and smiled. "Chick is the company Midas. He gets arthritis every time he has to sign a check." Her lips were still glistening scarlet, and there was a sultry curve to her mouth as she met Johnny's eyes.

Clark sighed, sat down again and pulled a large flat check-book toward him. He started filling in a blank check.

Johnny added, "Were you, by any chance, here in the office last night about the time I was up here?"

The bookkeeper held his pen poised above the check-book and looked at Johnny Saxon. "No," he said. And added, "Why?"

"The police have been checking on me," Johnny told him. "They don't seem to want to take the elevator operator's word for the time I left . . . *before* Sam was murdered. I might need more alibi."

"Christ! That's hot!" said Clark. "You a suspect yourself, and now Jasper Ward hires you to investigate."

Johnny looked around for an ashtray, finally dropped the cigarette on the bare floor and stood on it with his shoe. He said, "Ward hired me to find Dulcy Dickens. That's what I'm getting paid for."

Clark looked at him sharply. "What's happened to her?"

"She's disappeared, that's all."

"Oh, my God!" The bookkeeper's voice was shrill. "And I just sent her a check!"

Two men walked down the hallway past the office. Johnny could hear their voices clearly. One was saying, "And so you'd better put a red dress on the dame. Make her a blonde, and this chain will be around her throat and a guy will have a shiv pressed against her heart. The hero is just coming in the door, two automatics in his fists, but he doesn't see the mad doctor behind the door. The doc has a vial of acid ready to throw at the hero . . ."

The voices trailed off along the corridor outside the small office.

Johnny Saxon looked at Kay and pretended to shudder. "Sounds like a cover for *Horror book*," he commented.

"It is."

"Don't they ever use anything but a red dress on the girl? They've been using red for years."

"This one'll be different," Kay laughed. "It will be torn to shreds."

"Exposing plenty of thigh," added Johnny.

"Exactly."

"Jesus!" Johnny snorted. "Do you wonder I got sick of writing that stuff? An editor would give you a cover like that and then ask you to write forty thousand words built around the scene."

"Well, it helps to buy cake," Kay pointed out.

Johnny said, "I remember a title I used once. *The Condemned Wore Red.* It was about a girl involved with spies——"

"Listen," the bookkeeper interrupted, "you'd better get busy and locate Dulcy. She's our star writer. Good God, if anything happens to her——"

He held out a long check. Johnny read it, folded it carefully and put it in his pocket. He winked at Kay, commenting, "This is better than writing bang-bang."

"You'd better find Dulcy," Clark said.

Kay was frowning. "What do you imagine has happened to her, Johnny?"

He shrugged. "That's something I'd like to know."

"You're a hell of a detective," said the bookkeeper.

Johnny looked at him. "Maybe you're a better one. Who murdered Sam Sontag?"

"How do I know!" Clark's lemon eyes flashed. "I wasn't in the building last night." His eyes went from Johnny to Kay.

And the girl said, "If that's supposed to be an implication——"

Johnny said, "He means me baby."

But at the same time he noted the slight tenseness of the girl's slender, tall body. He remembered how it had been Kay Leigh's silhouette he had seen with Sontag's last night, etched against the frosted glass of the publisher's office door. He wondered just how much the girl might know. Had her warm ardor a few moments ago in Sontag's office been merely an act to win him over to her side . . . just in case she got in a jam later on?

He didn't think so. He thought she was emotional and sincere.

Johnny swung toward the door. He flicked his hand in a salute toward Clark. "Thanks for the contribution, friend."

"You damn well better earn it!" the bookkeeper said sharply. Kay followed him out.

Down the hallway, he paused and asked her, "I want to make a phone call. Is there a private booth——"

"There's one in the reception room." She nodded down the hall. "You can go out that way." They continued along the hall, and at the doorway to Sontag's office—*her* office now—she put her hand on his arm.

"Johnny . . ."

He waited. Her eyes were velvet-shadowed in the dimness of the corridor. "Johnny, you don't think that I had anything to do with . . . I mean, last night——"

He squeezed her hand. Her fingers were cool. "Of course not, kitten." He told her his room number at the Palace Towers. "If you get any lead on Dulcy, call me there or at the office."

She nodded, leaning toward him slightly. "Johnny, I want to help you . . ."

Somebody came out of the art department doorway. Kay immediately moved back from him. He said, "I'll see you later," and left her.

The reception room was deserted. But an operator was on duty behind a sliding glass panel. He went over to the open window and said, "Can you get me a number?"

"Sure," the girl said. She stopped her gum-chewing. "What number do you want?" She was a synthetic blonde with pink cheeks and a pouting mouth. She looked at him frankly with intimate blue eyes.

Johnny repeated the number of the *I Never Sleep* agency.

"You can take it in the booth," she said, nodding across the reception room.

"And listen," he added significantly, "I'd appreciate it if you wouldn't listen in."

The girl's eyes widened. "I like that! What do you think I am, anyway . . ."

Johnny grinned. "All right. All right." He leaned his elbows on the window opening. His voice lowered confidentially. "But *somebody* listens in, Mabel. I was wondering . . ."

"If somebody does," she snapped, "I don't know

about it." Her red-tinted lips pressed tightly against her teeth. "Besides, the name isn't Mabel. It's Fanny."

"I was afraid of that," said Johnny. And when the operator looked at him sharply, he had the five-dollar bill folded between his fingers and was holding it just above the switchboard. He said, "Maybe you can remember if somebody just by chance happened to be on another line when Jasper Ward called me a while ago in Sontag's office?"

The girl's round blue eyes hovered between the bill and Johnny's lean face. They came back mostly to his face, and seemed to be more impressed by what they saw there.

"Well . . ." she hesitated.

He let the bill fall. Immediately one of her hands covered it.

The girl looked beyond him, to make certain no one had entered the reception room. She narrowed her eyes as she looked at Johnny, as though she was getting ready to tell him some dark secret. The expression did not make her look any more intelligent.

"He asked me to plug him in on the line any time someone called Mr. Sontag's office."

"Who?" Johnny prodded.

"The one whose office you were just in."

His eyes flickered. This little floosie herself had been listening in, too!

"You mean," he said, "Chick Clark?"

The girl nodded. She looked a little scared.

Johnny exclaimed, "Well, I'll be damned!" He was remembering how worried the little bookkeeper had acted when he'd heard that Dulcy Dickens was missing . . . whereas all the time he had known. He had know because Jasper Ward had talked about Dulcy on the wire. What the hell, Johnny thought! He wondered if Clark had been ordered by sleek Jasper Ward to keep a check on things . . . or was the bookkeeper suspicious of Kay Leigh?

He looked down at the blonde. She smelled of cheap perfume. "Thanks, baby. Now you can get me that number."

He moved across the room to the phone booth, closed

the door behind him and waited with the receiver to his ear.

A moment later Moe Martin was saying "Gosh, have I been worried!"

"Worried?"

"I've geen trying to reach you at the Palace Towers, and there wasn't any answer. I left Dulcy Dickens contract up there in our room."

"Why in the hell didn't you go back and get it?" Then, with a start, Johnny asked, "You haven't heard from her, have you?"

"No. Not a word. Look, are you at the hotel now?"

Johnny told him he wasn't.

"How will I get that contract?" Moe asked worriedly. "I don't want to lose it."

"What do you mean, how will you get it?"

Moe explained sadly, "I went out for a paper after you left. I was afraid to ask for the key again at the desk. I thought maybe they might say . . ."

"Say what" demanded Johnny. "It's our room, isn't it?"

"But we haven't any money to pay for it!"

"The hell we haven't." Johnny figured swiftly. "We have two-hundred and thirty-four dollars." He explained about the retainer from Jasper Ward.

There was no answer from the other end of the line. He rattled the hook, figuring that Moe had been cut off. Then Moe's amazed voice, "*Yoiks!*"

Johnny said, "I'll be down in a little while, but in case . . ."

"Wait a minute."

"What's the matter now?"

"I almost forgot. We've got another client. A man named von-something-or-other is coming up here to see you. You'd better get right down here."

"Von what?" Johnny asked.

There was a pause. He could hear Moe shuffling papers near the phone. Then, "Baron von Elman, he gave his name." He added excitedly, "It sounds like somebody important." "So hurry!"

Johnny said, "For God's sake wipe some of the dust off those chairs," and hung up.

CHAPTER TEN

TWENTY MINUTES later, Johnny Saxon got out of the elevator on the thirteenth floor of the building on lower Fifth Avenue and hurried down the hall to the office of the *I Never Sleep* agency. He was reaching for the doorknob when he heard the commotion from beyond the door.

Something heavy was being dragged across the room. Chairs scraped. He heard an object fall. A shadow moved across the frosted glass, disappeared, quickly appeared again. There was another thumping sound.

Puzzled, he carefully opened the door.

Johnny stared. A massive, nicely grained mahogany desk had been set across one corner of the room. A single green blotter and desk-set adorned its polished surface. There was a swivel chair to match the desk. On the floor was a deep-piled rug of rich brown color. The three-foot-high stack of dust-laden manuscripts had disappeared. The room was clean.

Johnny turned as Moe Martin appeared from the inner office. Moe's bald head was moist with perspiration. He was slapping dust from his clothes.

At the sight of Johnny, his round, usually sad face brightened. "How do you like it?"

Johnny peered beyond his wide-set partner into the inner office. Louie Hart's overgrown body appeared from over the edge of the old roll-top desk, which had apparently been hastily rolled into Johnny's former sleeping quarters. Louie's features looked as though he had just emerged from a chimney. Dusty manuscripts had been hastily dumped into the inside room. They were on the cots and heaped in ragged piles on the floor.

Johnny turned questioningly to his stocky partner. "What the hell!" he said.

Moe was hurriedly smoothing out a wrinkled rug. He looked at Johnny, beaming. "Pretty swell, huh?"

"Where did you buy this stuff?"

"I didn't."

"But how——"

Moe was grinning happily. "I was talking to that girl who works for that sewing machine company down the hall. Mr. Turner—he's her boss—won't be back, until Monday morning."

Johnny's eyes narrowed. "And so?" He was beginning to understand.

"I told her we'd pay her five dollars for the loan of the stuff until tomorrow. We can move it back in the morning. Louie and I just got finished."

"*We'd* pay her?" said Johnny.

Moe looked startled. "Look," he exclaimed, "you've got that two-hundred dollars, haven't you?"

"A check," said Johnny. "And what's left out of Joe Rogers fifty over that. But we've got to live over the week-end. We can't cash this check until Monday."

"Maybe they'll cash it for you at the hotel," Moe offered brightly.

In the connecting doorway, Louie said, "Pretty snazzy, eh, boss?"

Johnny turned. "For Christ's sake, keep out of sight when this Baron von Elman arrives. You look like a tramp." He turned to Moe. "What time did he say he'd be here?"

"Four o'clock."

"It's four now," said Louie.

Johnny's speculative gaze went to the gaudy magazine covers still hanging on the office walls. His name sprawled across the covers made him shudder a little. "You'd better take those damn things down," he said to Louie.

The big young man grumbled. "Look, boss, them covers show what a great writer you were . . ."

"Take them down," said Johnny.

Still grumbling Louie removed the illustrations and carried them into the other room. Johnny closed the door behind him.

Moe, looking worried, rearranged an extra chair beside the desk. He placed another near the window. He sat down with a weary sigh. "I hope I've thought of everything," he said.

He jumped up again and hurried over to the hall door. He opened it a crack. "So we can hear him when he gets off the elevator, he explained.

Johnny sat behind the big desk, his feet resting on one of the pull-out shelves.

He said, "I wonder who this Baron von Elman is?"

Moe shook his bald head. "He didn't say over the phone. But he was awfully anxious to see you."

"What about?"

"He didn't say that, either." Moe's eyes worried. "I hope he's not another detective."

"Who ever heard of a cop with a name like that?"

"That's right."

"Before you left the Palace Towers," Johnny said, "was there any other word about that girl?"

"Who?"

"Dulcy, you fool! Who else would I mean?"

"Oh!" Moe said vaguely.

"Well?"

"No, she didn't come back at all."

"I didn't mean that," said Johnny. "Was anybody there looking for her? Was anybody there *at all?*"

Moe shook his head sadly. He sat looking out the window.

It was getting dark now, and it was snowing again. *Winter in Manhattan.* That's a good title, Johnny thought. Girls walking through the streets with fur-topped galoshes framing their pretty legs, dresses swirling in the wind or wrapped against slim legs; people hurrying home from offices, leaning into the icy blasts that faced the canyonlike side streets; lights coming on, flickering diamonds that chased away the drabness of night. Taxi horns bleating. News-boys huddled at street corners, flapping their arms, screaming, "Huxtra! Huxtra!" An ambulance yammering down the Avenue. People, weary people, pushing and cramming into subway kiosks like moles burrowing into the damp earth; others, fresh and bright, just starting the day. Heading for clubs and bars and restaurants. A pretty girl with a white evening gown held high about her slim ankles, being helped from a cab and running across to a cocktail lounge doorway. Gals and clean-shaven boys. Bums and prostitutes. A man without a hat standing in the gutter, waiting quietly while his leashed dog sniffs an automobile tire. A taxi rushing by, its tires making wet, sloppy sounds in the black slush. Mud splashing up. The dog owner cursing. "You louse!" Winter in Manhattan. People on an island. Millions of people. The pulse beat of a nation. Life. Glamour. Tragedy.

And somewhere in all this was Dulcy. Johnny thought of this, and there was a pain in his heart. Just a child, he thought. A child with green kitten eyes and lips that were a burning red. He remembered her voice, low, soft. "Shonny!" The way she had said his name, as though she had been repeating it to herself all her life. "Shonny!"

Somewhere I'll find you, he told himself fiercely. *I will. I will.*

His head throbbed. He looked at Moe, staring vacantly out of the window. Moe was saying, "Yeah, she sure was a nice girl."

Johnny swung to his feet. He lighted a cigarette and stalked up and down the room. "If we only had the vaguest idea where she could have *gone!*" he said. "But she was a total stranger here. She didn't know a soul. I don't even know where to *start.*"

"Yeah," said Moe, "that's what makes it tough."

Someone was coming along the corridor. Moe looked startled. "Psst!" he said, jabbing his finger at the door.

Johnny quickly sat down again. He pulled open the top center drawer of the big desk and hurriedly pulled out some letters that were carelessly piled there. He pretended to be busy reading. He wondered how a successful business man should look when he was reading.

There was a quiet knock on the door. Moe hurried to answer it. Someone said, "Mr. Sason? I'm Baron von Elman."

Moe was saying, "Oh, he's the one you want," and was leading the arrival across the office.

Johnny looked up from the letters. "Did you say Baron von Elman?" he asked.

The tall man nodded. Johnny stood up, reached across the desk, and shook hands. Moe was pulling up a chair. "Glad to know you," Johnny murmured.

"Mr. Saxon," Baron von Elman said formally, "I'm here on a very serious mission. I hope you can help me."

Johnny smiled. "Well . . ." He motioned to the chair that Moe had drawn up. His quick eyes ran over the man swiftly.

Baron von Elman looked like a successful banker in English tweeds. He wore pince-nez spectacles attached to a black silk ribbon. He was tall, spare, and ruddy-featured. When he laid his hat on the desk, Johnny noted that his hair was iron gray. He sat there wiping his spectacles with a clean handkerchief, replaced them again, then looked at Johnny Saxon.

"I understand," said the stranger, "you used to be a writer."

Johnny smiled. "That's a matter of opinion. I've sold some stories, yes."

Moe said, "He sold every pulp publishing house in New York! He was terrific." Moe had drawn up a chair just as though this were a family gathering.

"Ah!" said the Baron. "Then you do know this—er—pulp business background, Mr. Saxon?"

Johnny nodded. "I know most of the publishers."

"And the writers?"

"A number of them."

"Good!" said Baron von Elman. "Then I think you are the man I want."

Johnny waited. He wondered what the man was leading up to.

"You see," Baron von Elman continued—Johnny would have guessed his age at close to sixty—"I'm looking for someone who has been associated with this same—what you call—pulp business. A writer."

Moe cut in, "We know plenty of them. I'm a literary agent myself. I . . ."

"My associate," Johnny smiled, giving Moe a look. He prayed Moe wouldn't shoot off his mouth about *some* of the would-be writers he had taken on.

"Then I can speak freely?" the Baron asked, indicating Johnny's partner.

"Absolutely."

"Mostly, I'm interested in your ability as a detective. I've heard of you. And just this morning you were recommended by a young lady who works for the Sontag Publications." Baron von Elman leaned forward toward the desk. "You heard about the murder last night?"

"It's still quite a mystery," Johnny said.

"You knew this Sontag person?"

"A little. I never did any business with him. He was a chiseler."

"So I understand." The Baron shrugged. "Well, it's not him I'm interested in. Now about this writer . . ."

"Who did you say the young lady was that recommended me?" Johnny interrupted.

"A Miss Kay Leigh."

Johnny's eyes raised. He made no comment.

"And this writer person?" he prompted.

"A girl," said the Baron, "named Dulcy Dickens."

Before Johnny could stop him, Moe groaned, "Oh, gosh!"

Baron von Elman was looking at the literary agent's worried, sad features.

"Don't tell me you know this girl?"

Moe jerked his head. "Yes, we do. I mean . . . we did! That is . . . we just met her and then she disappeared!"

"It's like this," Johnny explained. "A friend—a publisher—asked us to meet Dulcy Dickens upon her arrival at Grand Central last night." He didn't mention that Joe Rogers and Jasper Ward had both *retained* him to locate the girl. "Shortly after she checked into the Palace Towers, she disappeared. That is about all anyone knows about her." He met the man's intent, cool gray eyes. "You are acquainted with her, Baron?"

"No. I've never met Dulcy Dickens."

"You're a publisher?"

"No."

"And yet you're interested in finding this girl?"

Baron von Elman nodded. His features were tense.

"It's so important that I find her," he said quickly, "that I'll gladly pay you five thousand dollars if you locate her . . . alive, naturally."

"Five thousand dollars!" Johnny thought he had misunderstood.

"That's correct."

Moe had a sudden fit of coughing. Above the handkerchief that he quickly held to his face, his eyes were startled and enormous.

Baron von Elman stood up, unbuttoned his heavy tweed ulster and pulled out a wallet. "I want you to give my case precedent over anything else you might be working on. Understand, it is urgent. You *must* find that girl!"

He counted out five one-hundred dollar bills and dropped them on the desk. "This," he said, "will convince you that I mean business. May I have a receipt?"

Johnny yanked open a drawer of the borrowed desk. His hands were trembling. He tried to act nonchalant.

The first thing that he grabbed was a pamphlet. "*Is There A Sewing Machine In Your Home?*" He pushed it aside. There were typewriter ribbons, clips, pencils a can of 3-in-1 oil in the drawer. And a photograph signed, "Love from Dotty." Dotty was lying on a beach, and she was wearing a one-piece bathing suit. She had large buttocks.

Johnny quickly shut the drawer. Moe was passing him something, saying, "I think our secretary reordered receipt books this morning. Use one of these cards."

It was a calling card that Moe must have had just printed. The name and address of the *I Never Sleep* agency was neatly engraved on one side. Johnny's eyes flickered.

Flipping the card over, he scrawled a receipt for the five-hundred-dollar retainer. He stood up.

"I'll get to work on this immediately, Baron. By the way, where can I reach you?"

"I live at the Murray Hill Hotel on Park Avenue. You can reach me there. Or leave word." He picked up his hat and buttoned his overcoat. "Good-day, gentlemen."

Johnny accompanied him as far as the hallway. "You

can rest assured that I'll leave no stone unturned," he promised.

He closed the door and came quickly back into the room. Moe gasped, "Christ! Five hundred dollars!"

"Get Louie ordered Johnny.

Moe swung open the door to the adjoining office. Louie Hart almost fell flat on his face.

He had been squatting there with his eye to the keyhole, obviously watching what he could of the proceedings.

"Is he gone?" Louie wanted to know.

Johnny nodded. "Listen, kid," he snapped, "and listen fast. You're being promoted."

"Promoted!" Louie's dark, close-set eyes widened.

"From now on you're a partner in the agency. Now here's what you do. You got a look at the Baron?"

Louie jerked his head. "Through the keyhole. When he came in."

"Fine," said Johnny. "Listen, did you ever shadow a man?"

"Sure!" said Louie. "I trailed a guy once that I was gonna shoot. But he died of pneumonia first."

Johnny frowned. "For God's sake, don't shoot the Baron. I want you to see where he goes, what he does, who he really is. Get it?"

"Yeah, boss."

Johnny had his hand on the hallway doorknob. He opened it a crack, listened. They all heard the elevator doors just closing. "All right, get going. Hop another elevator to the lobby. Call me at the Palace Towers later."

Just as Louie was going out the doorway, Johnny grabbed him by the coat, slid his hand beneath the overgrown young man's left armpit. He removed the small automatic and dropped it in his pocket.

Louie whined, "Gosh, boss . . ."

"You're *not* going to kill anybody!" said Johnny.

Grumbling, Louie hurried down the hall.

Johnny went to the desk, picked up the five one hundred dollar bills, placed them with the bank roll that was accumulating in his pocket.

Moe eyed the money hungrily. "Do you know the last time we had steak?" he reminded.

"We'll eat at the hotel."

"We're going back there?"

"Naturally. This place depresses me. Besides, we can check on Dulcy while we're having dinner in our room."

"Dulcy!" Moe was puzzled.

"I'd forgotten all about her luggage," Johnny said.

CHAPTER ELEVEN

AT THE Palace Towers, Johnny called Room Service and had dinner served in their room. It was a good dinner. They had onion soup, fresh green salad, planked sirloin steak, baked Idaho potatoes, and apple pie a-la-mode. They also had double Scotch-and-sodas before the meal. And because the drinks made him feel better, Johnny Saxon ordered two more double Scotch-and-sodas afterwards. He had been without sleep for hours, and his eyes ached, but the meal and the liquor made him feel better.

In fact, he felt so much improved that when the waiter was removing the table and dishes from the room, he suggested that a bottle of *Haig and Haig* be sent up. Moe thought it was a good idea, too.

Moe was sprawled out on the bed, his shiny bald head propped up by a pillow. For once, he did not look worried. He said dreamily, "I've got a magnificent idea, Johnny."

Johnny had a thick Manhattan telephone directory balanced on his knees and was bent over a page. His finger ran down a column of names. "Yeah?" he answered absently.

."I can get a full-page ad in *Writers Digest* for only a hundred and twenty dollars," Moe said. "Imagine the clients that would bring me! Why, in a month . . ."

"Humn," Johnny mused. "Baron von Elman isn't even listed here."

". . . I'll bet at least five hundred people would answer an ad like that I'll charge only the beginners for reading their stories . . ."

"He must have a private listing," said Johnny thoughtfully.

"Who're you talking about?"

"Baron von Elman. He hasn't any phone."

"Maybe that guy's a phoney," Moe Martin said.

"Phonies don't go around handling out one hundred dollar bills!"

Moe gave a start. "Maybe the bills are phoney!"

"You would have heard about it by now if they were. I used two of them to pay advance rent on this room and Dulcy's."

Moe groaned. "Why pay in advance? There might be a fire!"

A bellboy arrived with the bottle of *Haig and Haig.* Johnny opened it, poured the boy a drink. "Good luck," he said, and took a drink himself. He gave the bellboy a dollar. Moe, watching from the bed—he was too stuffed with food to get up—grimaced as Johnny gave the tip.

When Johnny had been writing steadily, he had made a minimum of a thousand dollars a month out of the pulps. He had never been considered cheap. He liked to spend money. It made him feel good, because he liked money. It made him feel good, because he liked nice things. Just being in this kind of a hotel made him feel good now. The delicate, cream-tinted walls of the room, the blue drapes at the windows, the subdued light of the floor lamps, the built-in ivory-colored radio . . . these things were nice.

He took another drink.

Johnny sat staring at the phone on the table; suddenly got up and walked over to it. He picked up the receiver and said, "Can you get me Long Distance?"

Moe's eys had been half closed. He opened them wide again and lay listening.

Then Johnny was saying. "I want to put through a call to New Orleans. I want to speak to anyone listed under the name of Dulcy Dickens." He spelled it out. "D-U-L-C-Y . . . D-I-C-K-E-N-S. I don't know the street address," he added.

He gave the hotel room number and said, "I'll wait you call me back."

Moe eyed Johnny worriedly. "The hell!" he said. "That call will cost dough."

"What you lack is imagination," said Johnny. "You have no vision."

"What do you mean?"

"The money we've been advanced so far is only chicken feed . . . compared to what we'll collect if we *find* that girl."

"I never thought of that!"

"Do!" Johnny said.

He felt very good. In fact, he felt pretty damned

splendid. Ideas pounded through his brain. First, though, he remembered Dulcy's baggage. Yes, that was it. He had been going to examine the bags that she'd brought with her to the hotel. Perhaps there would be some clue.

Moe asked, "Why did you call New Orleans?"

"There's a chance," Johnny told him, "that Dulcy's mother might know someone in New York. Some place where Dulcy might have gone. Maybe since Dulcy Dickens became famous, they've had their phone listing put under that name, instead of her real one, whatever it is."

"Maybe they haven't got a phone, at all," Moe said glumly.

"All right, pappy, all right," sighed Johnny. "Make it tough."

He was holding the room key in his hand . . . the key that he still carried to Dulcy's suite across the hall. Leaving the room door ajar in case the phone should ring he crossed the corridor and entered the girl's suite. "He turned on the lights. Dulcy's bags were still there; everything was the same.

Johnny felt like hell the moment he was in the room. He thought of Dulcy and her small, sweet face, and the soft dimples that were in her cheeks. He remembered her in the tan coat and tan galoshes and the beret, tilted against her windblown hair. He remembered exactly the way she walked. There had been her voice, low and soft and sort of breathless; the bright and eager way she had looked at you.

He muttered, "Dammit!" and walked back across the hall and got the *Haig and Haig*, and a tumbler from the glass shelf above the bathroom wash bowl. He returned to Dulcy's room, placed the bottle on the floor beside the bed and sat down. He tried to think.

Had there been some little thing she might have said that would prove a clue to her whereabouts now? He couldn't remember anything. All he could think of was her eyes, smiling, bright and happy. *That lovely kid,* he thought.

He took a drink. Then he got up and put one of the traveling bags on the bed. He opened it. And felt a little guilty doing so. Yet he had to search for any slightest thing that might tell more about her.

He placed things in neat piles on the bed. Shoes. Dresses. Sheer silk stockings. Fluffy silk underthings that were like spun, tinted air. He felt like a curious husband taking a peek at his bride's trousseau. Funny, he had never thought of what it was like to be a husband. At least, not until he met Dulcy. She was a child . . . and yet she made you think of doing noble things. He wondered if any of the girls he had ever gone out with considered him noble.

There was a set of crimson-red pajamas. The tops were monogrammed, "D. D." There were blue pajamas. And yellow ones. And a sheer, organdie nightgown. He held it up against his shoulders, and it just reached to his knees.

In the partially open doorway of the room, the girl giggled.

Startled, Johnny looked up.

The girl was standing there, swaying a little, supporting herself against the door jamb. She was looking at him out of slightly bleared eyes. She was tall, blonde, and vividly pretty.

Johnny dropped the night gown and moved toward the door. "I think you must have the wrong room . . ."

The blonde's hand left the door molding; she took a step forward and stumbled. She fell into Johnny's arms.

If he had not held on to her, she would have gone flat on her face.

She looked up at him. "Have you seen Charlie?" She was drunk.

The blonde's face was just below his own, as she clung to his shoulders. She had red lips, a voluptuous mouth. She smelled of jasmine.

"Is Charlie your dog?" Johnny asked.

"My husband," said the blonde. She hiccoughed.

He felt suddenly as though he were holding dynamite.

"Your husband!"

"Yes."

She was still swaying against him. He didn't want anyone to see the blonde in his arms like this, but he knew if he let got of her she would fall.

"Listen," he started worriedly, "I'm sorry I can't help you . . ."

"We're on our honeymoon," she said, "and now I've lost him. I've lost Charlie?"

"Well look, lady, he isn't here. I don't know where Charlie is. Maybe you got the wrong hotel. What hotel were you stopping at?"

"It was a nice hotel," the blonde said somewhat vaguely. "With twin beds and there were a lot of hallways."

Johnny groaned.

"What'll I *do-oo?*" the blonde moaned. "We were on our honeymoon, and now I've lost him." She clung to him.

Johnny thought that if he had been on a honeymoon with a pretty blonde like this one, he never would have lost her.

The girl abruptly flung her arms around his neck and started bawling.

"Jesus!" he groaned.

Across the hallway, the telephone was ringing in his room.

Johnny managed to get the girl out into the hallway. He left her leaning against a wall. "Sorry, babe, but I can't stay with you." The phone was still ringing.

Moe had one eye open now, and was lying there watching the phone. "It's got a nice ring," he said. "We ought to ask them for one like that at the office."

Johnny made a dive for the instrument. "Why the hell didn't you answer it? It might be New Orleans!"

"That's what I was afraid of," said Moe glumly.

"Hello?" Johnny said, tensely. "Hello?"

And then, after the operator had checked on the room number, she was saying, "I'm sorry, but we can't find any telephone listed under the name of Dulcy Dickens in New Orleans."

Johnny murmured, "Well, thanks anyway," and hung up. He was frowning. "The hell!" he said.

"They couldn't get anybody?" Moe asked. He was sitting up on the side of the bed.

"No."

"Then we won't have to pay for the call, will we?"

The telephone rang again.

Johnny scooped up the receiver. "Hello?"

It was Joe Rogers. "What have you found out?" His voice was staccato and urgent. "Any word on Dulcy?"

"Not yet," said Johnny. "By the way . . ."

In the doorway of the room, a tall blond young man in a green suit said menacingly, "What the hell's the idea fooling around with my wife?" He glared at Johnny.

Johnny hung to the phone with one hand and made frantic motions to Moe with the other. "Look, mister, I don't even *know* your wife! And I don't want to. Scram!"

On the phone, Rogers said, "What the hell are you talking about?"

"I didn't mean you, Joe. Just a minute . . ."

Moe was saying, puzzled, "Who's this guy, Johnny?"

"*He* knows who I am!" said the young man in the green suit. He advanced with balled fists into the room. Johnny groaned. Moe looked worried.

"Dammit!" Johnny grated. "Throw him out!"

Moe got his wide shoulders against the stranger's chest and crowded him back through the doorway. The door slammed behind them. There was a lot of loud talking out in the hall.

Johnny said into the mouthpiece, "Okay, Joe . . . where were we?"

"Where were *you?*" demanded Rogers. "What was that bird shouting about his wife?"

"He had the wrong room," Johnny explained quickly. And then, "Joe have you ever heard of a guy named Baron von Elman?"

There was a brief silence at the other end of the line. "No-o," Rogers said slowly, "I don't think so. Why?"

"He's looking for Dulcy."

"You mean, he's some relative?"

"He doesn't even *know* her!"

"Then what the hell?" said Rogers.

"That's why I'd like to find out who he is," Johnny explained further. "I'm waiting for a call about him now. I've got someone shadowing the Baron."

Rogers said, "Well, listen . . . I phoned to ask you

about Jasper Ward. Is that skunk paying you to find Dulcy?"

"Well . . ." Johnny started.

"Look," Rogers went on, "the hell with that punk. You're working for me, get it? Find Dulcy. Find her dead or alive. You do that and I'll pay you three grand."

Johnny's eyes opened wide. He was thinking, What *is* this? How come so many people are suddenly so interested in Dulcy? Sure, the kid could write; she was good. But no publisher in New York was kicking through with three thousand dollars just to hang onto a writer. They could build up one of their regulars cheaper than that.

"You heard what I said?" Rogers was asking.

"Yeah," Johnny murmured, "I heard you."

"Well?"

"How are the police making out?" Johnny asked. "Have they got any idea what's happened to Dulcy?"

"Not yet."

"How about Sontag? Have they figured out who killed him?"

"No. Those lousy cops!"

"What's the matter?"

"They had me on the mat for three hours today. They wanted to know if I did it."

"Did you?" Johnny said.

Rogers gave a brittle laugh. "Hell, no. But I'm sorry I didn't. That guy! That cheap chiseler!"

Johnny was silent a moment. Then, "Joe, what do you figure is the connection between Sontag's murder and Dulcy's disappearance?"

"I'd like to know. That's why I'm asking you to find out. First, though, *locate that girl*. Remember, there's three thousand fish on the line if you do. Now get busy!"

Johnny said, "Okay, pappy, okay," and hung up. He started for the bathroom.

The telephone rang again.

Before Johnny could answer it, Moe Martin—looking slightly disheveled—came back into the room. He made certain that he locked the hallway door behind him.

"What a time *I* had!" he said.

Johnny grinned. The phone was still ringing. "Did you find the guy's wife for him?"

"Some drunken blonde!" Moe exploded. "She got the wrong floor. To hear the guy talk, you'd think I'd had her in *here*!"

"I'll bet you would have liked to!"

Johnny answered the phone. It was Louie Hart.

Louie's low, husky voice said, "Hey, boss, I found out about that Baron von Elman."

"Yes?" Johnny prompted.

"You'll never guess about that bird," said Louie. "What I mean, the business he's in."

"Well," Johnny said rather impatiently, "what is it?"

"Hell, all he's got is a secondhand bookstore on Forty-seventh near Madison!" Johnny's bright eyes were thoughtful.

CHAPTER TWELVE

LOUIE HART hung up after his call to Johnny Saxon and felt in his pocket for the piece of paper on which he'd written the other telephone number. His big, ungainly form almost filled the booth, and he had a difficult time moving. But finally he got the paper held up in his left hand, the nickel in the other. He dialed the number.

A Filipino answered, and Louie asked to speak to Jasper Ward. He gave his name. There was a pause, and then Jasper Ward's brittle voice was saying, "What is it?"

"This is Louie Hart."

"I don't know any Louie Hart," snapped Ward.

"Look," said Louie, "I work for Johnny Saxon. I work for his agency."

"Oh!"

There was a short silence. Then, "What do you want?"

"There's something I gotta talk to you about, Mr. Ward."

"Well . . ." The voice at the other end of the wire hesitated.

Afraid that the man was going to hang up on him, Louie Hart quickly added, "Remember Les Hart?"

"What about him?"

"Les is my brother, Mr. Ward."

There was no reply to this. Louie's dark eyes were worried. He thought perhaps Ward had hung up on him. "Listen, are you still there . . ."

"Yeah, I'm still here," said Ward crisply. "Where are you now?"

Louie named the drugstore on Lexington, from which he was phoning.

"All right," said Ward. "Hop a bus and come up in half an hour." He gave his apartment address.

"Say, thanks, Mr. Ward!" exclaimed Louie, and hung up.

He stepped out of the booth and his chest swelled. He felt very good indeed. This was swell. This was big time stuff, having an appointment with a big shot like Jasper Ward.

Outside, it was snowing. Louie turned up his coat

collar and headed north along Lexington. He had plenty of time to walk to Ward's place. He was used to walking, working for that punk Moe Martin. If he'd wanted to ride, most of the time he'd had to pay his own carfare.

Ward's penthouse apartment was on the seventeenth floor of an exclusive East Side address off Lexington. The living room rug was a rich tan, and the modernistic leather-upholstered furniture was cream-colored. One entire side of the big room contained nothing but block glass windows, and beneath these were built-in bookcases, a phonograph-radio, and little shelves for knick-knacks. There were mirrors on all the other walls.

Ward moved restlessly up and down the long room, his built-up heels making sharp tapping sounds as they touched the polished floor beyond the rug. He was wearing a powder-blue suit, a purple shirt and yellow tie. There was a faint odor of jasmine about him. He suddenly stopped his pacing, leaned against the mantel and looked sharply at the man seated in one of the deep leather chairs.

"Then you're certain of your facts about Joe Rogers?" he asked. His slim, tapered fingers drummed restlessly on the mantel edge as he studied the man in the chair.

George Howie was a big man, and fat. His carelessly worn clothes were unpressed. A roll of fat overhung his shirt collar. His face was round and heavy. His eyes were small and shrewd and calculating. He nodded, and said:

"I've worked for that guy five years. I ought to know. Look at the information I got for Sam Sontag . . ."

Ward nodded impatiently. "Yes, yes; I know." The smooth, cold pallor of his face was unreadable. "How many of those magazines did you work on?"

Howie shrugged. "All of them, at one time or another."

"Then you know the circulation figures?"

"Naturally."

"All right, I want to get them," said Ward. "Especially on the books that are going good. The hell with the duds. We'll bring out duplicates of the good ones. We'll use the same authors . . ."

"But they're signed up with Joe Rogers!"

Ward's low, smooth voice sharpened. "So what? We'll offer them higher rates. After they turn in a few stories, we'll cut them again. We'll cut them down to half a cent."

George Howie raised his fat bulk in order to reach for the drink that was on an end table beside the chair. His small eyes watched the sleek racketeer. "You said 'we'."

Ward nodded. "Starting one week from Monday, you work for Sontag Publications. You work for *me*."

"Say!" Howie's eyes brightened. "That's great!" Then his eyes swiftly narrowed again. "And the salary . . ." he started, cautiously.

"Double what you're getting now." Ward's strange, light-colored eyes flickered restlessly. "Now here's what you do. In the next week, get the addresses of every one of Rogers' lead writers. Find out any new books he's got planned. Line up some of his artists." He moved away from the mantel, stepped to a liquor cabinet across the room, mixed another Scotch-and-soda and brought it over to the big man sprawled in the chair. "How about second-serial and reprints?"

Howie handed Ward his empty glass and shook his head. "Joe Rogers never publishes a reprint. He plugs that fact on all his contents pages. Every story published is a new story that has never appeared before."

"Okay," said Ward. "Then we will beat him to it. Find out what rights those authors sold him. Get a list of all stories that we could get second rights on. We'll give the authors five bucks a story. It'll be gravy for them. They'll be glad to unload some stuff that appeared five years or so ago."

Howie studied his drink a moment, tossed it off, then looked at his well-dressed host. "I suppose you know Rogers is going to fight? He's a tough baby to deal with. He won't take this lying down."

Ward nodded. He moved toward the foyer, indicating that the interview was over. "That's why I want you to get every figure you can. If you can ball up things over there before you leave, so much the better. I want to put that piker out of business. From now on, Sontag Publications is going to lead the field."

The big man stood up. His clothes fit his heavy frame loosely. He asked, "What about that dame who worked for Sam . . . that Kay Leigh? You going to keep her on?"

Ward's pale eyes were thoughtful. "For awhile, yes. She knows the business inside out." He frowned. "I think Sam let her do *all* the work for him!"

Howie picked up his overcoat and hat from another chair, and followed the distributor to the door in the foyer entranceway. Ward paused with his hand on the doorknob. His eyes, half veiled, studied the big man. "What do you figure about Dulcy Dickens?"

"What do you mean?"

"Do you think Rogers is hiding her out?"

Howie paused with one arm inside his overcoat sleeve. "I doubt it. Rogers is almost nuts trying to find her. He's got that Johnny Saxon looking for her."

"The hell he has!"

Howie nodded. "That dame's the hottest thing in the love magazines today. If Rogers finds her, and gets her writing feature novelettes for those two new books . . ." He looked carefully at Ward. "Of course, if anything should *happen* to him——"

"You mean . . . to Rogers?"

"Yeah. Don't think we're not going to have some competition with that baby. He's going to fight. But if he wasn't around . . ."

"What are you suggesting?"

Howie smiled thinly. His small eyes were sharp. "Well, you've got connections. The right kind. You might think it over."

Ward opened the door. "It's an idea," he said quietly. Then, "Goodnight. Keep in touch with me next week. I want to know *every* move Joe Rogers makes. And if you find out anything about Dulcy Dickens . . ."

"I'll let you know," said Howie, and went down the hall.

Ward closed the door. His thin pale face was thoughtful as he pulled a scented handkerchief from his coat sleeve and slowly wiped his hands.

A Filipino house man in white mess jacket came through the living room and into the foyer. He said, "Man named Louie Hart waiting to see you in lobby."

"Tell them to send him up." Ward watched the servant's retreating figure halfway across the room, then added sharply, "Wait. I'll meet the kid in the lobby. Tell him I'll be right down."

It was a small bar just off Lexington Avenue. In the rear of the place were booths lined with heavy red leather cushions. There was a small dance floor. A string orchestra sat on a slightly raised platform at the rear of the room.

The lighting was soft and indirect, with a color scheme of red and silver. The place catered to a select clientele.

Louie sat in the booth opposite the sleek-looking distributor and his close-set eyes were wide with wonderment. He had just finished his third drink; his flushed, bloated face was sweaty.

"Jeez, this is class, huh?" he said.

"Like it?"

"You bet, Mr. Ward!"

Louie's eyes roved across the dance floor, centered on the girl dancing with a tall, blond chap. He avidly watched the smooth sway of the girl's round hips. His bright eyes never went higher than the girl's waist.

Ward followed Louie's gaze, glanced at the girl with disinterest, then studied the young man thoughtfully. He said softly, "You stick with me and you'll see better things than this. Now in regard to Johnny Saxon——"

Louie tore his gaze away from the girl.

"Yeah?"

"You keep right on working for Saxon, see? I want to know everything he does. I want to know if he . . ." Ward paused, frowning. "Are you getting all this, kid?"

Louie jerked his head. He took another swallow of the drink. "Sure thing, Mr. Ward," he said quickly.

"All right, then. Never mind that girl over there!" He counted off items on his slim fingers. "I think Saxon knows something about Sam Sontag's murder. First, find out all you can about that. Then, this Dulcy Dickens dame. Watch every move Johnny Saxon makes. I'm also interested in Baron von Elman. Why the hell is that secondhand book dealer looking for Dulcy? Find out that. Report to me every day."

The waiter passed the table. Ward ordered another

drink for Louie. He was drinking nothing himself but was letting Louie make up for it.

"Now, about Les . . ." he went on.

"My brother's still in the Tombs," Louie said sadly. His voice was getting a trifle thick.

"I know," said Ward.

"You two used to be friends, didn't you?"

Ward nodded. "We worked on a couple of jobs together. I'd do a lot for Les. Any day. Maybe I can do something now."

Louie's eyes lighted with admiration. "Say! You really think . . ."

"Kid, you play ball with me, and I'll see what can be done about Les. You stick close to that Johnny Saxon, but don't let him know you're working for me." He reached in his hip pocket, removed a wallet, slid two bills across the table.

Louie's eyes widened when he saw the denomination of the bills. He said, "Christ, Mr. Ward, for that kind of dough, I'd even shoot somebody for you. Is there anybody you want——"

"Never mind that!" Ward snapped. His pale gray eyes were hard. "You just do what I tell you."

"Sure," said Louie.

He had two more drinks. When they stood up to leave, Louie swayed a little. His gaze went to the dance floor, watching the girl who was still dancing with the blond-haired fellow. Louie's tongue ran over his lips, then he gave vent to a deep sigh.

Watching him, Ward sized up Louie Hart's heavy shoulders, his large, overdeveloped body. He gripped the young man's arm and steered him away from the dance floor, toward the street exit.

"You can do better than that," he said.

"You mean——" Louie's bleared eyes centered on his new idol with admiration.

"Sure," said Ward. He led the way out to the street, waved down a cab, helped Louie inside. To the driver, he gave his own apartment address.

It was still snowing hard, and traffic crawled through the streets.

CHAPTER THIRTEEN

JOHNNY SAXON sat up in bed with a sudden start. The hotel room was cold, the chintz curtains billowing inward at the open windows. Johnny turned on a light beside the bed and looked at his watch. It was just 1:00 A. M.

Beside him in the bed, Moe Martin's shiny bald head was the only thing showing beneath the blankets. Moe stirred uneasily, grunted, "What the hell's the matter with you?"

"I've got it!" Johnny exclaimed. He swung out of bed and started shaking Moe.

His partner turned over, stuck his round, sad face partially from beneath the covers. He blinked one eye balefully against the glare of the table light.

"You got what?"

"An idea!"

Moe groaned. He rolled over on his stomach again. "Look," he said, "this is a very nice bed. It's the first bed with a mattress I've slept in for months. And I've only been in it an hour. Now why can't you turn off the light . ."

"I just thought of it!" said Johnny. "The trunks!"

Moe's voice came half muffled from beneath the covers. "What trunks?"

"Dulcy's!"

For ten seconds, Moe lay still, thinking. Then he sat up, pulling the covers around his shoulders. His wiry black hair stood out at grotesque angles around his bald pate.

"How do you know she had any trunks?" he demanded sleepily.

"She said she had two trunks coming by express today," Johnny Saxon pointed out. "So . . . where are they?"

Moe looked dazed. "I don't know. Where are they?"

Johnny moved across the room, pulled down the windows, then started hurriedly dressing. "That's what I intend to find out," he said. "Find the trunks, and maybe we'll find Dulcy. At least we'll find out more about her. Come on, get up!"

Moe touched his toes to the cold floor tentatively. He finally stood up. He was wearing a long white nightgown. If there had been a cord tied around it, he would have looked like a monk.

Grumbling, he dressed. Ten minutes later, they were riding an elevator to the lobby.

"How do you know where to find any trunks?" Moe asked.

"We'll inquire at Grand Central. That'll be a good place to start."

Moe was still dubious. "What good will it do finding her trunks? Dulcy is the one we want." He shook his head sadly. "If I only had her name on that contract——"

When the elevator door slid open at the lobby, Johnny was urging his partner forward. Outside, they looked for a cab. One quickly rolled up from the nearby corner, and they climbed in.

It had stopped snowing, and it was colder now. Slush in the streets had frozen, and crunched beneath the tires. Moe sat back in the corner of the seat with his shoulders hunched down in his coat collar, his derby pulled low on his head.

At Grand Central, Johnny directed the driver, "Drive down to the baggage room."

A moment later, he was questioning a clerk.

The man shook his head. "You gotta have baggage checks to get any trunks," he said wearily.

"I realize that," said Johnny. "You see, " he said glibly, "I was supposed to get those trunks for a young lady. She gave me the baggage checks, and now I've lost them. So I thought if you had her name and address, you might be able to trace them."

Johnny took a dollar bill from his wallet and dropped it on the counter. Moe frowned, looking at the bill.

The clerk eyed the bill, and his eyes brightened a trifle. Then he shook his head. "Mister," he pointed out, "we only got three hundred trains a day arriving here. Half of them have trunks on 'em. So how the hell am I supposed to find any trunks without baggage checks?"

Johnny Saxon wasn't ready to give up. "Well, I can

tell you where these trunks were from, and whose name was on them. That might help a little. They would be in the name of a Miss Dulcy Dickens, and . . ."

He stopped as he saw the narrowing of the clerk's eyes.

"Did you say Dickens?" the man asked.

Johnny nodded.

"What the hell you trying to pull?" the clerk demanded sharply. "Those trunks were called for tonight."

Johnny stared. "But if they didn't have the checks—"

"They had 'em, all right. They was sent down by messenger, an' we sent the trunks out like they asked."

"Sent *where?*" Johnny prodded.

The clerk eyes him suspiciously. Moe Martin looked suddenly worried. He touched Johnny's arm, whispered, "Maybe we'd better forget about those trunks!"

But Johnny had taken something from his pocket. It was a shield, and he flashed it briefly. He lowered his voice and said confidentially, "I think you'd better give us that address, bud."

The man's eyes looked startled. He quickly went to a desk, returned with a file board on which were clipped papers. "We're only too glad to help the police department," he said. "Let's see . . . Here it is! They were delivered to East Forty-eighth Street." He gave Johnny the street number. "If I had known you gentlemen were detectives——"

"That's okay," said Johnny, quickly jotting down the number. He left the dollar bill lying on the counter, and led the way back to the waiting taxi. He gave the driver the address on 48th Street.

Riding uptown, Moe asked, "Where'd you get the police shield?"

Johnny grinned. "I picked it up one day for an artist. He was doing a cover for a lead story I'd written. I remember the title of that one: 'Shield 322'. It was a good yarn. I got three hundred dollars for it." Johnny took the police shield from his pocket and looked at it. "It's an imitation, of course, but not bad,"

Moe shook his head. "I hope you don't get us into any trouble with that thing."

It was only a matter of moments until they were riding east on 48th Street. The driver slowed, swung into the curb. He said, "Here it is, bud."

Johnny was on the edge of the seat, staring ahead. "Wait a minute!" he said. He was watching the other taxicab that was just pulling away from the curb.

Moe asked, "What's wrong?"

"That guy who just got into that cab," Johnny said tensely. "Something familiar about him." To the driver, he ordered, "Follow that Yellow!"

Already the first cab had lurched away from the curb and was halfway to the corner. It swung south on Madison. By the time Johnny's cab had reached the corner, the light had changed to red. He swore. There was a police prowl coupe parked just across the corner.

"You'd better wait," he warned.

When they finally got started again, and swung south on the Avenue, they saw the first cab turning east again on 46th Street. Johnny suggested, "Just trail that fellow, driver. I want to see where he goes."

At each click of the meter, Moe shuddered. There was already a charge of almost two dollars showing.

By the time they swung left on 46th Street, the other taxi was already well ahead. The driver of Johnny's cab pushed his hack to the limit, but he could not seem to cut down the intervening distance.

He took chances and jumped red lights at Third and Second Avenues. But the first car was already turning southward on First Avenue, a long block ahead. The driver shook his head. "That bus is one of them new DeSotos," he said. "Those babies can move!"

And he was correct. By the time they swung into First Avenue, there was no cab in sight. A couple of trucks lumbered along the wide street. That was all.

Johnny frowned. "Swung around a couple of side streets," he suggested. "Whoever was in that cab knew we were following him. That's why they gave us the slip."

Johnny's driver cruised around several blocks. But they picked up no trail of the Yellow. Moe was still watching the meter worriedly.

"All right," Johnny said finally, "drive back to that 48th Street address. I guess we've lost them."

A few moments later the driver pulled up again before the darkened building on the side street. They climbed out. Moe whispered, "Don't have him wait. This isn't the only cab in New York. We can get another when we're finished."

Johnny paid the bill—$3.45—and gave the driver a dollar. "At least you tried," he said.

Going up the shadowy steps of the old brownstone, Moe said gloomily, "Anybody would think we were millionaires!"

They were in a dark vestibule. Johnny felt around for a bell button, finally lit a match and saw the small sign: NIGHT BELL. He pushed the button.

They waited.

Finally a light went on inside and someone was coming along the hall. Johnny warned, "Let me do the talking." The door opened and a gaunt, cadaverous-looking man in an old bathrobe and slippers stood frowning at them.

"Well?" he asked.

Johnny edged inside the doorway. He gave the man a quick glimpse of the police shield and said, "We're looking for someone."

The police shield had magical effect. "Oh sure," the gaunt man said, and started leading the way back through the wide, oak-paneled hallway. "We had one come in today that's unidentified."

Moe shot Johnny a puzzled glance. And Moe was sniffling suspiciously. There was a peculiar odor about the place.

"Mr. Baumhofer—he's the owner here, you know—is down to Atlantic City at a convention," the man explained, looking over his shoulder. "But if there's anything I can do——"

He opened a door at the back of the hall. Cool air struck Johnny Saxon's face. He paused just inside the doorway while the tall man fumbled along the wall for the light switch.

"I'll show you the one I mean," the fellow was saying.

The lights came on brilliantly.

And Moe gasped, "Yoiks!" and looked suddenly pale.

Johnny stared.

Tables in the room contained more than half a dozen corpses.

The attendant shuffled across the room and indicated one of the tables. "This is the one," he said. "The city sent it today. No identification. We get a certain percentage of these you know." The man's deep-set eyes brightened as he looked at Johnny Saxon. "Of course, if you officers can identify the body, and we can locate some relatives, we can collect more than the city's small fee for a funeral. In that case"—his hawklike, lean features grinned. knowingly—"well, we're ready to play ball, you know."

"I understand," said Johnny. He stepped up beside the man to get a look at the corpse. The odor of formaldehyde in the room had made him slightly nauseated.

The body was that of an elderly man of indeterminate age. The features were gray-yellow, and withered. Johnny turned quickly away. No, that's not the one," he said.

Moe looked like he was going to be sick. He had already started back toward the hall door.

Johnny said, "I'll just take a look at these others. The one we're looking for was a woman . . ." He moved around the room, inspecting the bodies.

Moe looked back sharply, giving his partner a curious, sickly glance.

"I don't think it would be any of these others," said the gaunt attendant. "They're all regular deaths and we have the names . . ."

Johnny nodded, continuing to inspect the bodies. He gave a sigh of relief when he saw that all six corpses were those of men. The thought had occurred to him just a moment ago that maybe Dulcy Dickens was dead; that perhaps she was in just such a place as this. He felt miserable.

On the way out, he asked casually, "There's another

thing. We'd like to check on some trunks that were delivered here tonight."

The tall, bony-looking man stared at Johnny. "Trunks?" There were no trunks sent here, officer."

Johnny frowned. "You're positive?"

The attendant nodded. "Positive. I've been alone here all evening, and I can assure you that——"

"All right," Johnny said. He was a pretty good judge of character, and he was convinced that the man was speaking the truth.

He followed Moe toward the vestibule door. Just as they were leaving, the gaunt man said hopefully, "If you ever have any . . . er . . . customers, we could give you ten percent."

Johnny turned and looked at the man. "Ten percent?"

The fellow nodded. "Take a Baumhofer Deluxe Burial, for instance. That's our special. We only charge two hundred and fifty dollars for that funeral. So if you ever know of anybody, we could give you twenty-five dollars if they took that funeral."

"I'll keep you in mind," said Johnny and went out. When the door had closed behind him and Moe, he said with a shudder, "Christ! The guy's a ghoul!"

Moe said, "Let's walk. I don't feel so good."

They both moved through the night in thoughtful silence. Finally Moe remarked, "It's funny about them trunks."

Johnny said: "Whoever got those trunks probably figured that someone else might be looking for them too. And so he could have picked that address as a blind, waited there until they were delivered, then paid the express man to take them somewhere else. That would throw anybody off the trail."

"You think maybe Dulcy's dead, and somebody got hold of her baggage checks?" Moe asked glumly.

Johnny's jaw set grimly. "Don't keep saying that!" he said sharply.

He tried to tell himself that Dulcy was all right; that she was alive and well somewhere in the great city; that he was going to see her again.

The air was clear and cold now. Overhead the stars were bright and sharp in a clearing sky. It occurred to him that today was Sunday. Sunday in New York, when the entire city would relax, when there would be none of the rush and noise of a week day. The kind of a peaceful day for lovers to meet.

In a few more hours, couples would be having breakfasts in warm, cozy apartments. They would be lounging around in pajamas, reading the funny papers. Sunday in New York.

But there was no peace in Johnny Saxon's heart. He kept walking. The chill crept through his overcoat, and he felt cold and empty and miserable.

CHAPTER FOURTEEN

BENEATH A CASEMENT window overlooking Central Park, steam hissed faintly. It was warm in the apartment, and intimate. Empty coffee cups and pieces of toast were on blue china plates, on the coffee table in front of the low, comfortable divan.

Joe Rogers turned away from the window and watched Hanna, seated on the couch, busy sorting over large black-and-white illustrations. The artboard squares lay on the floor, on the divan, on her lap. Hanna picked up two double-spreads and studied them critically. She said thoughtfully, "If I remember correctly, the girl in this story had blonde hair. We'll have to speak to the artist about it."

Rogers said, "Yes," absently and continued to look at Hanna. She was wearing red lounging pajamas which set off the yellow hair that brushed her smooth shoulders. Woven Mexican sandals covered her bare feet, which were partly tucked up under her.

She picked up another illustration, her cool green eyes quickly catching each detail. "This fellow Meyers isn't bad," she said. "We might try letting him do the next cover for *Lightning Detective.*"

"Sure," said Joe. He took his hands out of his pockets and moved across the room. His gray, pleasant eyes saw the warm red of Hanna's lips, the soft curve of her mouth.

Brushing the illustrations aside, he sat down beside her, pulling her slender figure toward him. "Baby, *must* we talk shop?"

Hanna put her slim fingers on his shoulders. "Darling! This art work was supposed to be okayed yesterday. But you were tied up with those policemen asking questions."

He kissed her lightly on the nose.

"Don't mention cops, baby."

"But——"

"Don't mention illustrations."

"But you haven't okayed them!"

"*You* do it, pet. Tomorrow. This is Sunday, remember. The only day we ever have together."

Her body was warm beneath the lounging pajamas.

There was a slight flush to her smooth fine cheeks. He put his arms around her and pulled her down on the divan beside him. "Take a memo," he said, grinning.

"Yes, Mr. Rogers."

"Joe loves Hanna. See that it is placed on Miss Hanna Carter's desk first thing in the morning."

She laughed softly.

"Anything else, sir?"

"This," said Joe, and found her lips. For a long moment, she lay very still against him. He felt the pressure of her firm, round breasts. She was trembling a little.

"You're beautiful," he whispered against her cheek.

"Darling——"

"Happy, sweet?"

She moved her head up and down. Her soft hair brushed his face.

"It's been a long time, hasn't it, baby?"

"Five years, Joe."

"Five precious years."

"Yes."

Her lovely green eyes held soberly on his mouth. Her hand touched his cheek, lingered there. "You can be sweet, Joe."

"I love you so, baby."

"I know," Hanna murmured.

They lay there in each other's arms, and outside a car moved occasionally through the street, and a horn blew, and the voices of children playing in the snow in Central Park lifted on the crisp morning air.

But in here, in Hanna's apartment, it was warm and quiet and intimate.

"Let's stay in all day," Joe suggested.

"If you want darling."

"Do you mind, honey?"

"Silly! Have I ever?"

She laid her warm cheek against his, and her arm crept around his neck.

In the kitchenette, the buzzer rang.

"Dammit!" he said, and sat up.

When Hanna came back from answering the buzzer, her eyes were worried. She had put on a robe.

"Joe," she said quickly, "it's that D. A.'s assistant—Small——and Nick Willis from headquarters."

"What do they want?"

"They're coming upstairs."

Rogers exploded. "Can't those guys even knock off on Sunday?"

Hanna was biting her lip. "You could wait in the bedroom. They needn't know you're here."

But he was straightening his tie and coat. "They probably saw me come in. No telling how long they have been hanging around."

Hanna looked upset. "But if they should say anything. I mean, about Ann. They might go to her——"

Joe's gray eyes flickered. "I'd like to see them try it." He squeezed her hand reassuringly. "Besides, what if they did? To hell with it! She knows, anyway."

"Yes, but——"

There was a knock on the living room door. Hanna went to open it.

Plump, well-fed A. A. Small marched into the room, followed by tall Captain Nick Willis. The D. A.'s assistant placed his hat carefully on a table and put on his most patronizing air.

"Ah," he remarked in his tinny voice, "I hope we are not interrupting."

Rogers grimaced. "You know you are!"

Big Nick Willis slouched into a chair and balanced his derby on his knees. His eyes merely raised a little at Roger's remark.

Hanna sat down on the edge of a straight-backed chair. She appeared taut and nervous. Joe let the sleek D. A.'s assistant remain standing, and sat down again.

Small stood in the middle of the room, carelessly fumbling with the black ribbon of his pince-nez. His casual gaze went from Hanna to Rogers.

"We've been doing a little checking up," he said easily. "We've found out there are quite a few people who . . . ah . . . disliked Sam Sontag, the publisher who was murdered Friday night."

"You're telling us!" Joe said.

Small again glanced from Rogers to Hanna. "In fact,

various people were pleased to see him put out of the way, weren't they?"

Rogers frowned. "Are you asking us or telling us?"

The D. A.'s assistant shrugged. "Just commenting," he said. His manner was casual and disarming, but it did not fool Rogers. He was thinking, *He's found out something. He's not kidding me.*

"This girl," said Small, "this Dulcy Dickens . . . has anyone heard anything from her yet?"

"No," Joe said.

"How about Johnny Saxon?"

"What about him?"

"He's looking for Dulcy Dickens too, isn't he?"

"Perhaps he is."

Small's fingers slid up and down the black ribbon of his pince-nez. "I should think you would know," he said. "Didn't you hire him to locate Dulcy?"

"All right, I did," said Rogers a little sharply. "Is that a crime in this state?"

"Oh, no, no!" said Small easily. "I was just asking."

Hanna was fumbling with a small lace handkerchief which she held in her lap. Rogers saw Willis glance at the girl occasionally. Hanna's legs were not quite covered by the robe which she hastily slipped on when the headquarters men had been announced; in fact, the slim, firm mold of her legs was visible through the red lounging pajamas.

Willis caught Joe's glance, looked guilty, climbed to his feet and sought an ash tray in which to flick the ashes that had collected on his cigar. He finally located a tray and carried it back to the chair with him. He said nothing.

The D. A.'s assistant continued, "You arranged to have Dulcy Dickens come to New York, didn't you?"

"You asked me that yesterday," said Rogers.

"Did I?"

"Don't be so hard to get along with," said Willis, speaking for the first time.

Joe shrugged. "I'm tired of hearing the same questions," he said. "You guys ought to have them put on a record."

A trace of the casualness dropped from Small. For the first time, his eyes were sharp and alert and cold.

"Why is Dulcy Dickens so damned important to everybody?" he demanded.

"She's important to me," said Rogers, "because she's the best love story writer in the game."

"She was important to Sam Sontag too," Small pointed out.

"Sure."

"And so you were going to cross Sontag and sign her up yourself?"

Rogers smiled. "So what?" Any smart editor goes after a name writer. Put a name like Dulcy's on the cover and you can jump the circulation ten thousand copies in a single issue."

Small looked at Hanna as though for confirmation of this statement.

Hanna's cool green eyes met the investigator's. "Joe's right," she agreed. Her voice was low and controlled. "Besides, we were offering her higher word rates."

Small swung back to Rogers and shot another question. "There was no love lost between you and Sam Sontag, was there, pal?"

"I hated his stinking guts!"

The D. A. assistant's eyes raised a trifle. "Hated him enough to stick a shiv in his back?"

The tall, well-built publisher snorted with disgust. "For Christ's sake you can hate a guy without murdering him. Sam Sontag was a rat and a chiseler. He paid the lowest rates of any publisher in New York. He used every cut-throat method he could to get circulation. But I didn't kill him."

"*Somebody* did," said Small.

He picked up his hat, bowed to Hanna, and moved toward the hall door. Willis had been sitting with his eyes half closed. He got up now and followed.

In the doorway, the D. A.'s assistant paused and said, "We'll be seeing you."

Willis' broad red face screwed up in a frown. "Have a nice Sunday, folks." He went out.

Rogers closed the door behind them, leaned against it

and faced the girl. "Those guys!" he said. "Those lousy punks!"

Hanna's smooth features were a little pale. "Joe, you don't think they suspect *you*,"

He shook his head. He lit a cigarette and stared thoughtfully at the girl. "But they know something. What? I'd like to know. That little punk Small is smart as a fox. He's got something in his head."

He moved nervously up and down the room. Hanna's eyes were worried. She went to the window and stood staring down at the park.

And he knew, suddenly, that this day they had planned to spend together was ruined. He was upset and nervous. He crushed out the cigarette in a tray and went into the bedroom for his overcoat and hat.

Hanna followed him quickly into the room. "Joe, you're not leaving so soon!"

Looking at her lovely face, he felt miserable. There was a delicate heady fragrance about the expensive perfume she was using, and she looked very young and very fresh in the bright red lounging pajamas. He cursed himself that the arrival of Small and Willis had upset him like this. But it had, and that's all there was to it. He didn't want to hurt her, but it would be better if he went now. He put his arm gently around her shoulder.

"See you in the morning, baby." He kissed her on the cheek. "Maybe I'll be in a better mood then. I'm sorry."

Hanna looked at him quietly, "You're thinking perhaps they'll tell Ann!"

"To hell with Ann!" Joe said. Ann was his wife. "Maybe I'll tell her myself!"

"Has she ever said any more about going to——" Hanna hesitated.

"To Reno?"

"Yes."

Joe shook his head. "It's that damnable streak in her," he said grimly. "She doesn't love me, and she knows I don't love her. It's just as though she wants to make us suffer for all that time she spent in a wheel chair. For something I'm not even *responsible* for! You know, you can get to hate a person for something like that!"

Hanna looked startled. "You mustn't say that, Joe," she said.

"It's true. Why doesn't she get the divorce? Why doesn't she do what she's promised to do for years? At least, she could make *us* happy!"

Hanna held his arm. "I'm happy, Joe. I've told you that. I'm always happy when I'm with you."

He held her against him. "I know it, baby. But it still isn't fair to you. Look at all the times you are *alone*. That's the part."

"Well," Hanna said quietly, "perhaps some day . . ."

He nodded. He picked up his coat and hat again, kissed her once, almost fiercely, and strode toward the living room door.

He went out.

Hanna stood there, her eyes misted, and the apartment was very still and empty around her. She thought of a Christmas Eve, and the morning that followed, that first time Joe Rogers had ever stayed there. She knew that nothing, *nothing*, could ever make her stop loving Joe

She was crying . . .

CHAPTER FIFTEEN

JOHNNY SAXON got up from the table, sighed contentedly, and followed Kay Leigh's tall, lovely figure toward the living room. "There's nothing like a home-cooked meal," he commented. "I haven't had a dinner like that in months." Then he added significantly, "in fact, sometimes I didn't have dinner." He thought of the electric plate in the back room at the office of the *I Never Sleep* agency, and of the countless cans of beans that had been heated over that make-shift stove.

Kay paused at the bottom of the two steps that led down into the sunken living room. She looked dark and beautiful in the subdued light from the shaded floor lamps, the indirect light shadowing her olive complexion. She picked up a silver cigarette box from a table, opened it, held it out to Johnny Saxon.

"Smoke, darling." Her flashing dark eyes were half veiled in the light. "Why don't you take off your coat and be comfortable? Let's not be formal!"

"That's an idea," he said.

Johnny tossed his coat and vest to a chair. Kay curled up in a deeply upholstered chair, let her cool fingers rest lightly on his hand as he held a match for her. Her deep eyes lifted to his. "I feel like a well-fed, contented kitten," she said with a sigh.

Johnny smiled. The cigarette tasted good. Blowing smoke thoughtfully through his nostrils, he remembered the questions he had come here to ask Kay. But they could wait a few moments. It was nice being here. Outside it was dark, and lights were coming on in the Village. Kay's apartment was in one of the older houses off Washington Square, but the rooms had been fixed up nicely. There were Persian scatter rugs, and brightly covered chairs, and on little corner shelves funny doo-dads like miniature cats and dogs and things.

Kay was wearing something close-fitting and sleekly black, and her long black hair was done up behind her head. Her lips were orange-red against the rich smoothness of her skin.

"She said, "Like a drink?"

"Does a duck swim?" said Johnny.

"There's some liquor on the pantry shelf. You'll find ice cubes in the refrigerator." She sighed lazily. "Look around out there and see what you can fix up."

Johnny went through the apartment to the kitchen. He opened cupboards, found some glasses, then located the liquor in the pantry. He selected a bottle of *Black and White.* Loosening one of the ice trays in the refrigerator, he carried it over to the sink and ran it under the warm water. It was nice doing these things again. He remembered when he had been selling stories to every pulp market in New York. Often he had knocked off on a Sunday afternoon to relax just like this.

A Sunday Afternoon, he thought. That was a good title. Only trouble was it had been used in the movies a few years ago.

He dumped the ice cubes into a bowl, filled the tray with water and replaced it in the refrigerator compartment. He found a siphon of soda, and soon had tall, well-spiked drinks ready.

Johnny was just turning away from the sink, the glasses in his hands, when he stumbled over the small, heavy dish that was on the floor. It slithered across the black and white linoleum and brought up with a thud against the baseboard. He put down the drinks and looked to see if the dish had broken.

But it was all right. He was just placing it up on the sink—there were some scraps of canned salmon still left in the dish—when Kay appeared in the doorway behind him.

"Having trouble, darling?"

He grinned.

"That's the first time in my life I almost lost a drink!"

Kay nodded to the dish that he had almost broken. "It's Michael's!"

"Michael?"

"The cat. He's asleep in the bedroom."

They went back to the living room.

"To us," Kay said, raising her glass.

He nodded. His eyes held Kay's over the rim of the

glass. Her eyes were shining, and he thought he detected a slight flush in her cheeks.

This time she sat down on the Chesterfield, and he took the arm chair she'd been using when he went to the kitchen.

Johnny stared thoughtfully at his glass.

And he said, "How do you think things will go at your place without Sam Sontag around?"

"Oh, I forgot to tell you!" Kay exclaimed. "Jasper Ward called me up this morning."

"About what?"

"Remember George Howie, one of the editors over at Rogers Publishing Company?"

Johnny nodded.

"He's coming to work for us in about a week. Ward's putting him in Sontag's place."

Johnny frowned. "Joe Rogers is going to love that!"

"I can imagine."

"Have you ever met George Howie, baby?"

Kay shook her lovely head.

"A first-class heel. A two-bit punk whom I've long suspected of selling information about Joe Rogers' business."

Kay sipped at her drink. "The kind you can't trust behind your back."

"Or in front of you, either! You won't like working with that guy."

Kay murmured softly, "Darling, get me another drink."

He was back in a few moments. There was something else on his mind. "About that knife . . ."

Kay shuddered. "Must we?"

"There's something I want to know," Johnny said. "The police found the knife wiped clean of fingerprints. Have you got any idea of what that means, honey?"

Kay looked up at him. Her mouth was sultry and moist from sipping at the drink. "What?" she asked casually.

"It couldn't have been a crime of passion. Anyone stabbing Sam Sontag during a fit of rage, would have been too wrought up to think about wiping off the knife."

Kay's eyes raised.

"So two to one it was a premeditated murder. It was carefully thought out in advance. It was timed to the exact moment when Sam Sontag was momentarily alone in his office—even though there were other people in the building."

Kay said, "But that still doesn't tell you who did it?"

"No," Johnny said with a weary sigh, "it doesn't. But there was something else I wanted to ask you——"

"Darling . . ." Kay stirred lazily on the couch. "How about another drink?"

Johnny took her glass and went out to the kitchen again. He tossed off the remainder of his own highball. He was feeling pretty good. It was just the kind of a winter's day to lounge around a warm apartment and get pretty well crocked. But there were still those questions he had come here to ask Kay . . .

When he came back into the living room, Kay was smoking another cigarette and watching him languidly. Her hand held his firmly this time as he passed her the glass. He smiled down at her. She certainly had a nice figure, it occurred to him. The way she was sitting brought out the soft curve of her smooth hips. Kay pulled him down beside her.

"Must you sit over there all by yourself?" she demanded. She looped her arm through his and pressed up against him. "It's nice being alone with you, Johnny."

He finished half the drink and set the glass on the rug near his feet. He squinted across the room at one of the miniature monkeys on a shelf. He wasn't certain if there were two monkeys or one. About three quick drinks always affected his vision this way. He supposed it was the first impact of the alcohol. After a while his eyes would be all right.

He looked at Kay and grinned. "How do you feel, honey?"

"I feel swell."

"So do I."

"It's kind of warm, isn't it?"

"Yeah, it is."

She raised her red, sultry mouth. He wasn't sure

whether he kissed her or she kissed him. Anyway, it was nice.

She was smiling. "This is better," she murmured huskily.

He was trying to remember what it was he had wanted to ask her. Then it came to him.

"By the way," he asked, "who ever gave Sam Sontag that hunting knife?"

"You'd never guess, darling."

He looked at her. Her moist lips were parted, and he could see her very white teeth. Her face looked hot.

"Who?" he prodded.

"Dulcy."

"The hell she did!"

"She sent it to Sam last Christmas."

"I've got an idea that——" he started.

"So have I," said Kay. "Let's have another drink."

They both went out to the kitchen this time. The ice cubes and soda. He clicked his glass against Kay's. He got another tray from the refrigerator. His movements were a little bit unsteady. In trying to dump the slippery cubes into the bowl, several spilled on the sink and scooted off to the floor. He bent down and picked them up, swaying as he moved back to the sink.

Kay said, "Darling, you're drunk."

"Who . . . *me?*"

She looked wonderful standing there.

Kay laughed. "Yes, you."

He poured out two drinks, not bothering to add ice cubes and soda. He clicked his glass against Kay's and said, "Hi, gorgeous."

"Hi, Johnny."

They drank.

Johnny said, "I'm as sober as a judge," and decided to prove it. He tightened his belt. "I'm in wonderful physical condition," he said. "I can touch my toes without bending my knees."

"Can you?" said Kay, smiling.

"Watch!"

He straightened up, then slowly bent forward from the

waist, holding his knees stiff. He almost went flat on his face.

Kay caught and steadied him. She was laughing heartily, and her face was flushed.

"Let's go into the other room," she suggested. "It's hot in here."

His arm was around her slim waist, and he was acutely aware of a heady fragrance about her that made his head whirl. At the top of the two steps that led down into the sunken living room, Kay paused, saying, "I'm so warm. I think I'll put on something cooler." She nodded to the bedroom door that faced the tiny balcony overlooking the living room; there was a wrought iron railing that separated the room from the balcony.

Johnny stood there holding to the iron railing. Kay left the bedroom door open. Her voice came out to him. "I'll only be a minute, darling."

He was feeling pretty drunk. He hoped she would not be too long.

Kay called out, "Johnny, see if you can snap this hook."

He went to the bedroom doorway. The soft delicate smell of powder and perfume touched his nostrils as he paused on the threshold. Kay was standing before the dresser, her hands reaching behind her in an attempt to snap some kind of hook that was part of the chiffon negligee she had slipped on. The negligee was pale yellow, and she looked utterly gorgeous.

Johnny stepped into the room and tried to find the hook that her slim fingers were seeking. He fumbled around for a while and then gave up.

"The hell with it!" he said thickly.

Kay turned around and faced him. "You're cute," she said.

"I'm a swell writer, too," said Johnny.

"Of course you are, darling."

"Some day I'm going to knock them dead with a book I'm going to write."

"You should write a book, Johnny."

"I'm a swell writer and I'm going to write a book."

"Of course."

Kay's arms were around his neck as she faced him. He

was conscious of her warm, slim body through the filmy negligee. Suddenly he had swept her up into his arms. She clung to his neck, giggling, and he carried her back toward the living room.

On the top step to the sunken room his foot slipped and they fell down the two steps to the floor. They landed in a tangled heap, holding to each other.

They were laughing.

Then Johnny became aware of a sound somewhere in the apartment . . . a persistent sound that finally began to bother him.

"What's that?" he asked.

Kay shrugged. "Just the phone, darling. Don't worry about it."

He listened to the jangling of the bell.

"It annoys me," he said.

Kay pulled him to his feet. "Forget the phone," she said huskily. Her eyes were bright.

But the phone kept ringing, and it jarred on his nerves—he was very sensitive that way—and finally he stalked across the room, up the steps and into the bedroom. The sound was coming from there.

He saw the ivory handset and picked up the receiver. "What the hell do you want?" Johnny said.

A man answered. "Who's this?"

"This is the *I Never Sleep* detective agency," said Johnny.

There was an exclamation from the other end of the line.

"I'll be damned! Johnny Saxon!" And then the caller added: "Is Kay there?"

"Naturally."

"Look," said the voice, "this is Chick Clark. I'm calling from a booth on the corner. I'll be right up. Tell Kay I've got to see her."

"Can't it wait until Friday?" Johnny Saxon asked.

"No," Clark said quickly. "I've got to see her tonight." He hung up.

"Nuts!" said Johnny, replacing the phone.

He went back to the living room. Kay was asleep on the divan.

She looked very lovely and very feminine, curled up with her arms around a pillow. Johnny went back to the bedroom, pulled a comforter off the bed, returned and carefully placed the cover over the girl's slim figure.

Somebody was knocking on the hallway door. The door was at the end of a small foyer at the end of the balcony. Johnny put on his vest and suit coat, located his overcoat and hat, then went and opened the hall door.

Chick Clark pushed into the room. His dark eyes were bright behind the thick-lensed glasses. He started to say "Where's Kay——" then paused. He saw Kay asleep on the divan. His eyes raised, and he looked at Johnny Saxon.

"I didn't know you two were such good pals," he said.

Johnny's gray eyes flickered. "Don't let it give you ideas."

"Now look," said the little bookkeeper, "I didn't say——"

"Well, don't!" snapped Johnny.

He took Clark's arm and then steered him toward the door. "You can't talk to her now. She's had too much to drink."

They went down the stairs, and outside in the cold, clear night, the fresh air hit Johnny like a kick from a mule. The sudden change made his head whirl.

"Call a cab," he said, swaying unsteadily.

He remembered riding uptown with the Sontag Publications' bookkeeper. He also remembered asking, "What was so damned important that you had to see Kay tonight?"

"Les Hart has escaped from the Tombs! He's somewhere loose in the city!"

For a moment, the name did not penetrate Johnny Saxon's brain. Then he straightened with a start.

"Les Hart! That racketeer who used to be associated with Jasper Ward?"

"Yes."

Johnny frowned. "Listen, you just don't escape from the Tombs. It must have been an outside job. Somebody helped him."

"That's what I'm afraid of!" The little bookkeeper was hanging to Johnny's arm.

"Afraid of what?"

"Look," said Clark tensely. "The police suspect Jasper Ward of Sam Sontag's murder. Ward is on a spot. He had every motive to bump off Sontag and then take over the entire business. More than once they fought about the amount of profit the books were showing. Ward figured Sontag was chiseling on him."

"He was probably right!"

"So now," continued Clark, "Ward's got to get the heat off himself. Since the police are watching him, he can't very well do anything himself. So what does he do? He gets Les Hart out of jail. He'll let Les do the job."

"What job?"

"Frame somebody else for the killing. Frame *anybody*—as long as Jasper Ward gets in the clear himself!"

Johnny thought about that for a while. Jouncing of the taxicab had made him pretty dizzy again. It was hard to think clearly. There was something else that was prodding at his mind, something that happened, or that he had seen . . .

The next morning, he awoke with a terrific hangover.

CHAPTER SIXTEEN

HE LAY FOR a long time with his eyes tightly closed. He was afraid to move. But even with his eyes shut he was aware that the room was bright with light; it was this that was making his eyes ache and his head throb. It felt like forty little devils were pounding on the back of his skull with sharp-pointed hammers.

Tentatively he opened one eye. And groaned.

Bright sunlight was pouring into the hotel room. The shades had been raised to the ceiling and the windows were opened wide.

Johnny Saxon swiftly shut his eye again and debated whether it was worth trying to get up or not. He decided that it was perhaps better to lie right here on his back and die!

But man is born with one curse—his conscience. Johnny's conscience kept telling him that today was Monday, and there were a number of important things he had to do. Besides, there was something else.

He vaguely recalled that, somewhere, he had picked up a significant clue. It had been something that concerned either Dulcy or the murder of Sam Sontag. Which, he could not recall. In fact, he could not remember what the clue itself was! Perhaps if he got up and took a shower he would be able to think better.

Johnny started counting slowly. His jaw set grimly, and at the count of ten he flung back the covers.

"Oh, Gawd!" he groaned, and fell back to the bed. His head had split into little pieces. He lay very quietly until the pounding in his brain subsided. Then, carefully, he moved one hand. Something crackled beneath the fingers that were holding the covers. He opened his eyes and looked to see what it was.

A sheet of hotel stationery had been pinned to the topmost cover. On it was Moe Martin's scrawled handwriting. Johnny read a column of notations that had been made on the paper:

Capt. Nick Willis phoned
Jasper Ward phoned

Kay Leigh phoned
I've gone down to the grill for breakfast
When are you going to get up?
(P. S.—*I took ten dollars out of your pants*)

The list of telephone calls gave him a start. He wondered what Moe had told everyone. Hangover or not he simply *had* to get up! There were things to do.

Johnny swung out, clutched the side of the bed for a moment, then moved toward the bathroom. He got into the shower as quickly as he could.

For fifteen minutes he let hot water needle his lean body. Slowly his head cleared. He switched the handle to "Cold" and slapped his chest furiously, dancing up and down and shouting as the cold water brought a pink glow to his skin.

Later, he rubbed himself vigorously with a heavy bath towel. He felt better. Wrapping the towel around his waist, he trotted out into the bedroom and called Room Service.

"Send up a double order of milk and ginger ale, mixed," he told the girl.

"You said milk and ginger ale?"

"That's right. Half and half. Two glasses."

"Yes, Mr. Saxon."

He stared around the room and wondered where he had put his clothes when he came in last night. He wondered how he had *got* in.

And then he saw the dry cleaner's paper bag hanging on the closet door. Ripping the paper down he saw that it was his gray suit—which Moe must have thoughtfully sent out to be pressed. It was a nice suit, the only good one he owned.

He located his new socks and shorts and an undershirt in the dresser drawer. Also some shirts. He selected a pastel gray shirt, a gray necktie with narrow barred stripes, and gray socks with a neat black clock. A waiter arrived with the glasses of milk and ginger ale while he was dressing.

The unusual drink had a marvelous effect. By the time he was putting on his necktie, he felt fine indeed. His stomach had stopped jumping. In fact, he was even hungry. The pick-me-up was one a tunnel worker had once told him about. Johnny had spent a whole evening in a bar with the sandhog, getting material for a short novel he'd been writing at the time.

Johnny was in the bathroom combing his hair when Moe Martin, looking excited and worried, came rushing into the room.

"Johnny!"

Moe's eyes were bright in his round, somewhat sad face. Johnny stood in the bathroom door, frowning at him.

"What's the matter with you, pappy?" he asked.

Moe was making frantic motions toward the hall door and talking at the same time. "Hurry up! Dulcy's room. Keys! Where are the keys?"

"You mean the keys to Dulcy's room?"

Moe jerked his bald head. "Yes, Hurry! *Somebody's in there!*"

Johnny was swiftly tense. "You mean . . . Dulcy?"

"I don't *know!*"

Frantically Johnny looked around the bedroom for his other suit. The key to the suite across the hall was still in that suit, he remembered.

"Where the hell's my clothes?" he demanded.

Moe leaped toward the closet. He came out with Johnny's other trousers in his hand. "Here!"

A moment later, the room key in his hand, Johnny was leading the way across the hall. Moe whispered, "I heard someone in there as I came down the hall."

Johnny put the key in the lock and quickly flung open the door.

A man, bent over one of the suitcases, spun. His cold, dark eyes held menacingly on Johnny.

"Les Hart!" said Johnny.

Moe gasped.

In the taut half moment that Les Hart stood very still, not a muscle in his body moving, it struck Johnny that there was a great deal of resemblance between the man and his younger brother—Louie. Only Les' face did not have that bloated look, and there was a shrewder intelligence in the depths of the man's unblinking eyes.

Les' right hand dived beneath the armpit.

Johnny moved with blurred speed.

His fist caught Les beside the ear, knocked him sprawling across the bottom of the bed. Les had a gun just clear of the hidden shoulder holster.

Johnny dived on the gun arm, twisted the wrist, straightened with the weapon in his own hand. He quickly backed off two paces and kept the man covered. To Moe, standing wide-eyed behind him, he said, "Close the door!"

Les stood up, rubbing his wrist. His eyes were narrowed and cold. Johnny remembered the gangster well; Les Hart's picture had been in the papers at various times in the past.

"Who sent you up here?" Johnny demanded.

Hart's eyes, half veiled, held a sneer.

"I'll tell *you*," said Johnny. "It was Jasper Ward."

Moe said, "Maybe I ought to call the cops!"

"Wait!" Johnny ordered.

He kept his eyes on the gangster. "What's Jasper Ward got you searching for?"

"Nuts," said Les.

Johnny shrugged. "Okay, wise guy, okay. We can call the law and have you sent back to the Tombs. Or we can play ball. I'm Johnny Saxon. Maybe in his hurry, Jasper Ward forgot to tell you he also hired me to work for him. Now let's play nice. Has he got you looking for Dulcy, too?"

Les relaxed slightly, though his manner was still wary. "I don't even know the frail," he muttered.

"Well, I'm glad of *that*," Johnny said. He held the gun steady on his captive's chest. "Then what were you looking for?"

Hart hesitated.

"Come, come," said Johnny. "Give!"

The gangster shrugged. "Okay. Ward figured the dame brought some manuscripts to New York. He wants them. He figures if the dame is croaked, he could still use the stories."

Johnny's gray eyes flickered. "Jesus!" he said sharply. "Sam Sontag was a bad enough chiseler. He practically stole stories at the rates he paid. What does Ward plan to do . . . hijack the stuff?"

"I didn't think to ask him," said Hart coolly.

Johnny heard Moe's hoarse breathing directly behind him. Moe stood with the phone clutched in his hands, ready to call the police.

A thought suddenly occurred to Johnny Saxon. "By the way," he asked quietly, "where did you get a key to this room? There were only two, and I had both of . . ."

Johnny remembered that he had left the second key in the dresser drawer, in his own room. He said over his shoulder, "Moe, step across the hall and see if there is a key to this room in the top dresser drawer."

Moe went out, closing the door behind him.

Johnny said, "I'm not a cop, Hart. So I'm not interested in turning you in. You're nothing but a small-time punk that isn't smart, that's all. And your kid brother is working for me. So I'll give you a break. I'll let you have a five minute start before I call the desk and tell them somebody was in this room." Johnny's eyes were cool and level and sharp. "But let me warn you. There's a nice kid named Dulcy Dickens somewhere in this town. I'm looking for her. Don't let me find you doing the same thing!"

Hart shrugged. "I don't tangle with dames, brother."

The door opened and quickly closed behind Johnny. Moe said worriedly, "That other key is gone!"

Johnny frowned. "When was Louie around last?" he wanted to know.

Moe said, "He came up last night looking for you. He hung around for about an hour, then went home."

Johnny snorted. "He stole that key for his brother here!"

Les grinned. "The kid's smart."

"Too smart!" Johnny stepped aside, broke the revolver, emptied the shells into his palm, and then tossed the gun to Hart. "You can get ten years in this state for carrying a gat," he warned. "Okay, scram. And don't come back!"

Les Hart was out of the door and gone in a second.

Moe said, "Why the hell didn't you call the police?"

"And get Nick Willis and that squirrelly D. A.'s assistant on our necks for being mixed up with Les Hart? We'll have enough headaches as it is. By the way, what did Willis want when he phoned this morning?"

Moe was sitting on the edge of the bed, patting sweat from his bald head with his handkerchief. The incident with Les Hart had had him worried for a few moments.

"He wanted to ask you something."

"What'd you tell him?"

Moe grinned. "I said you were out. I said you wouldn't be back until later this afternoon."

"What about Jasper Ward?"

"He wants you to drop around and see him today," Moe looked up at Johnny and he shook his head. "Boy, you sure were high last night!"

Which made Johnny remember. "And Kay Leigh?" he went on. "What did she say?"

"She wanted to know how *you* felt." Moe's forehead creased. "By the way, where were you last night?"

Johnny grinned. "What else did she say?"

"She just wanted to make sure you got home all right. She says to call her up at her office when you get time."

But Johnny decided that the call could wait. There was work to be done.

He locked the door to Dulcy's suite and led the way back to their own room. They were no sooner inside than the hall door burst open behind them.

Louie Hart stood there, his young face bloated and unpleasant. "Listen, you louses, where's Les?" His face was working.

Johnny took a step toward the large young man and then paused. He noticed something about Louie's dark, close-set eyes.

"He's gone," Johnny told him.

"Yah!" bellowed Louie. "You turned him in! You got him arrested! I saw a police car going down the street. . ."

Louie's features were suddenly ugly. He lurched forward, his hand dipping into his side pocket. "I'm gonna blast your stinking guts . . ." A small automatic appeared in his heavy fist.

Johnny hit him. He didn't pull his punch. Louie

sprawled backward to the floor, the automatic flying from his fist. Johnny quickly scooped up the weapon and dropped it into his own pocket.

Louie started climbing to his feet, glaring.

And Moe said, "After all I've done for you, you ungrateful punk!" He caught hold of Louie and started slapping him.

Johnny Saxon stood back, amazed. He had never seen his benign, always somewhat bewildered partner so emotionally upset. Moe stopped slapping the big young man, drew back his fist and let fly. Louie fell down. He was out.

Moe calmly walked to the bathroom, filled a tumbler with water, came back into the room and dumped the contents into Louie Hart's face.

Moe exclaimed, "That gun! He must have got it out of the dresser drawer, too, when he stole the room key. The gun was in there last night, right where you left it!"

Johnny nodded, watching Louie. The large young man was sitting up on the rug, sputtering, wiping water from his mussed clothes. He looked suddenly sad and beaten.

"I'm sorry," he muttered. "I guess I lost my temper."

Johnny helped him to his feet. Again he noticed Louie's eyes, the small contracted pupils.

"It might be a good idea," he warned, "to get over that yen to kill somebody. It's going to get you into trouble."

"I thought you had Les pinched," said Louie.

Johnny shook his head. "I caught him snooping around the room across the hall. But I gave him a break. Next time, I won't."

Moe said, "You try anything like this again, kid, and you're fired." He took a dollar from his pocket. "Have you been down to the office yet?"

Louie shook his head. Moe ordered:

"Well, get down there and see if there's any mail."

Louie shuffled out. Johnny stood there looking thoughtfully after him. After the door had closed, he turned to Moe and said, "That dumb kid's been using dope."

"Dope!"

"Didn't you notice his eyes? I'd like to know who got him started on the stuff."

"I wonder who did?"

"I've got an idea."

Johnny shrugged his shoulders restlessly, stepped across the room to the writing desk and sat down. "Look up the phone number of the New York *Times*. I want to call them and place a notice in their Lost and Found column."

"What did you lose?"

"Nothing. But I'm going to pretend I did."

Moe stared at him queerly, and Johnny explained, "We're going to put in an ad for a lost dog." He had written something on a sheet of paper. "How does this sound? 'Lost: Small white poodle. Answers to name of Kiki. Anyone seeing this dog, please call Room 3009, care of the Palace Towers. Reward'."

Moe was astounded. "That's Dulcy's dog!"

"You mean——"

"I mean I've picked up a clue." He sighed. "I don't know where she is. I don't know where the pooch is. But maybe if we find Kiki, we'll locate Dulcy."

Moe shook his head sadly. "It sounds screwy to me."

Johnny handed him the ad which he had written on the sheet of paper. "Call up the *Times* and have them insert this for three days running. Tell them to bill me here. Then there's something else we've got to do."

Moe put through the call, then looked up. "What?" he asked, in response to Johnny's statement.

"We're going to see that secondhand bookdealer—Baron von Elman."

CHAPTER SEVENTEEN

THE BOOKSTORE was on 47th, near Madison. Johnny Saxon and his partner walked, since it was not far from the Palace Towers. The sun had come out and the air was clear and crisp. Snow removal equipment blocked traffic on every side street. Sand had been spread on the slippery sidewalks and street crossings.

Johnny only took time to grab a sandwich and a malted milk at a corner drugstore. A few moments later, they came to a halt before the bookstore window.

It was not the type of secondhand place found further downtown, like the bookstores down around Greenwich Village. A few rare editions were displayed in the large show window. There were also several autographed letters.

"It looks like a classy place," said Moe. He glanced at the number of the building. His brow knitted in a puzzled frown. "You know, there's something familiar about this address!"

He looked past the store, noticed the alley at the end of the building. The alleyway cut through to 48th Street, a block beyond.

"Say!" Moe exclaimed. "That's it, this street address! It's exactly behind that funeral parlor on the next street . . . the place we visited Saturday night!"

Johnny did not show surprise. "I was wondering if you'd discover that," he remarked.

"You mean, you've already noticed it?"

Johnny nodded. "I think the man we saw getting into the taxicab in front of the funeral parlor Saturday night was Baron von Elman."

"You think *he* has those trunks?"

"Possibly. Having the trunks delivered to the address on the next street was merely a blind. Baron von Elman could have waited there for the express man, pretended he had given the wrong address, and thus intercepted the trunks."

"Where would he have gotten the baggage checks?"

"That's what I've been wondering," said Johnny.

"Why would he want the trunks, anyway?"

"I wish I knew. It might clear up a lot of things."

They had moved on past the bookshop, pausing in an adjacent doorway beyond the alley entrance. Johnny had noticed the name on the bookstore window. "The Book Nook," he said, reading the name. "That's the way it must be listed in the telephone book. No wonder we couldn't find the Baron's name listed."

Moe said, "It's funny he didn't tell us about it."

Johnny's eyes were thoughtful. "He had some reason for not wanting us to know he was in this business, if you ask me." He started back toward the store. "Come on."

"What are you going to do?"

"We're going to have a talk with the Baron, pappy."

Inside the store, several people browsed over books located on counters and on the many shelves. It was a long store, and there seemed to be plenty of books. Johnny's quick gaze noted that some of the books were in glass-enclosed racks and locked. He glanced at a couple of editions. He was no rare book expert, but from some of the titles he knew that the books were valuable.

A tall, thin-faced woman in a severe black dress and a white lace collar came toward them.

"May I help you, gentlemen?"

"We'd like to see Baron von Elman," Johnny said.

"I'm sorry, sir. He's out at the moment. Perhaps I can get you something . . ."

Johnny smiled. "I'd rather see him personally. I can wait."

The thin woman nodded toward the rear of the store. "Perhaps you'd like to sit down while you're waiting. You may use the office."

Johnny thanked her and led the way to the rear room, reached through a small archway in the back of the store. Moe remarked, "Say! I saw a book out there priced at two hundred dollars!"

Johnny nodded. "Some first editions are worth thousands. This isn't a bad racket." He grinned at his wide-set partner. "It's even better than being a literary agent."

"Well," Moe said hopefully, "maybe some day I'll discover a genius."

Johnny was prowling around the room, glancing at other glass-enclosed shelves that were back here. "Sure," he said, "maybe you will. But geniuses aren't appreciated until they are hundreds of years dead. Where would that leave you?"

The thought brought a startled expression to Moe's round face.

In one corner of the room there was a wide mahogany desk. Steel filing cabinets were against the wall behind the desk. Apparently this was Baron von Elman's office.

Johnny Saxon's restless curiosity led him over to the desk. He deliberately read some typewritten letters that were lying on the green blotter.

Moe looked at Johnny and then toward the archway. "Hey, be careful!"

But something else had caught Johnny's interest. It was lying on the left side of the desk, and looked not unlike a manuscript. It was quite thick and bulky.

"Let me know if anyone comes back this way," he said quietly to Moe, then stepped behind the desk and picked up the object.

It *was* a manuscript, written in a neat hand, in ink. The pages were yellowed with age. The copy was in French!

Johnny could read enough French to get the general drift of the story. His eyes went quickly down the page. They widened in wonderment. The writing, the mood, the feeling here was terrific. He glanced at the author's name at the top of the first page. Jean Beaumont.

He thumbed through the pages, his eyes alive with interest.

"Psst!" Moe hissed. He was standing near the archway, looking nervous and worried as he kept glancing from Johnny out into the store. "That clerk's coming this way!"

Johnny quickly replaced the manuscript, stepped across the room and picked up his hat from the chair where he'd dropped it. He started through the doorway just as the tall thin woman reached the rear of the store. She gave him a questioning glance.

"I'm sorry," he said smiling, "but I'm afraid we can't wait. We'll drop back later."

"Whom shall I say called?" the woman wanted to know.

"Well . . . ah . . . tell him it was Captain Willis, of

police headquarters," Johnny said on a sudden impulse.

The woman looked startled. "Ye-es, sir," she stammered.

Outside, Moe exclaimed, "Jesus!" You're going to get us in a jam. What was the idea?"

Johnny took his partner's arm, steered him up the street toward where he had seen a waiting cab. "I want to try a little experiment," he said.

"What was that you were reading?"

"A manuscript."

Moe's eyes brightened. "Was it any good?"

"It was in French."

"Who wants to read anything in French?"

They had reached the cab. Johnny opened the rear door, climbed into the back seat. "Don't start up yet," he told the driver quickly. "I want to wait for someone. You can put down the flag, though. We will pay whatever's on the meter."

Moe said, "What's the idea?"

"Wait."

They waited. Twenty minutes. From time to time the meter clicked. Moe stared at it in dismal fascination. Suddenly Johnny touched his arm and said, "There he is!"

Down the street, tall, well-dressed Baron von Elman was just going into the bookshop.

"What are you going to do now, Johnny?"

"I have an idea when he gets that message from the woman, he'll go out again. It's just a hunch. Anyway, we'll wait and see."

They did not have long to wait. Within a few moments, von Elman emerged hurriedly from the store, buttoning up his tweed overcoat and looking around for a cab as he headed toward the curb.

A taxi was cruising through the side street. He waved it down, said something to the driver, then jumped in the back. The cab rolled toward Fifth Avenue and swung south.

"All right," Johnny said to the driver. "Follow that cab."

Traffic was heavy on Fifth Avenue. The big doubledeck

buses slowed up other cars, and thus it was an easy matter to follow the cab ahead.

Moe frowned. "Where do you figure he's going?"

"That's what I hope to find out. I had a hunch he'd go out again when he was told that Nick Willis had been at the store."

"You mean he's going to see somebody?"

Johnny nodded.

"Dulcy?"

"No-o," Johnny said thoughtfully. "It couldn't be her. It's someone else. He probably didn't want to take a chance on phoning."

Moe sat back and sighed when he saw the meter change again. "I hope he's not going to Brooklyn!"

But they didn't have to trail the other car very far. In the Grand Central section it swung east, finally drew up before the building on the eighth floor of which were located the offices of the Sontag Publications. Baron von Elman paid off the driver and hurried into the lobby.

Moe stared. "Who would the Baron be seeing *here?*" he asked in amazement.

Johnny had ordered their own driver into the curb. He paid him off and started across the sidewalk.

"I can't even guess," he answered. Johnny, himself, seemed puzzled that the trail should have led here.

There were several banks of elevators in the Mauser Building lobby. A car stood waiting. But gray-haired Baron von Elman was not in it.

Johnny said, "He's probably gone up." He rubbed his ear for a second. "Tell you what, Moe. You'd better go back to the hotel. There might be somebody looking for us. I don't know how long I'll be." Johnny took a couple of bills from his pocket and pushed them toward his partner. "You need any money?"

Moe shook his head. "I've still got seven dollars and thirty-eight cents left out of that ten."

"My God!" Johnny gasped. "You sound like a cash register. Do you even keep track of the pennies?"

"I'm thinking of the room rent at the Palace Towers. Dulcy's suite alone is fifteen bucks a day. That advance you got won't last forever!"

Johnny patted him on the back. "Cheer up, Uncle. There's plenty more coming to us."

"*If* you find Dulcy!"

"I'm going to."

Johnny put the bills back in his pocket and stepped in one of the waiting cars. At the eighth floor, he got out, crossed the corridor and entered the reception room of Sontag Publications. He stepped directly to the receptionist's window.

"Hi, Fanny. Remember me?"

The blonde with the baby blue eyes was on the switchboard. "Oh, hello!" she said brightly. She was still chewing gum.

"How goes it, Toots?"

"Swell."

There were two men waiting in the reception room. One had a large art drawing propped beside his chair. The cover illustration was done in oil, and was gaudy and sexy. The other fellow must have been a writer; Johnny could tell by the hopeful, hungry expression on his thin features. He was holding a manuscript envelope on his knees. From time to time he sent expectant glances toward the girl's window.

Johnny was just leaning confidentially through the open window, to ask the blonde a question, when she got a call on the board.

"Yes, Mr. Burns," she said sweetly, "I'll tell him."

She smiled at Johnny Saxon. "Pardon me a minute." She looked past his broad shoulder and spoke to the thin young man holding the manuscript envelope.

"Mr. Terry?"

The young man leaped to his feet as though he'd been sitting on a coiled spring.

"Yes?" There was a hopeful look on his thin face.

"Mr. Burns says he hasn't had a chance to read your story. Call back next week."

The fellow's face dropped. "Well . . . all right," he said quietly. He turned and headed toward the door. His shoulders slumped now, and his face was no longer bright.

Johnny Saxon shook his head. How well he remembered that same feeling. He recalled the days when he himself had just started out. Tramping from one editorial office to another, leaving manuscripts, calling for rejections, trying to see editors.

"I'm sorry, sir, but Mr. Clinton can't see you today. Can you come back tomorrow?"

Of course I'll come back. I want to eat, don't I? Oftentimes walking all the way uptown from 8th Street, to save two subway fares and the price of a phone call. Waiting. And then, sometimes, the great day when *it* happened.

"You haven't done a bad job on *Contraband Corpses,* Mr. Saxon. We're putting it through at a cent a word. The check will be ready Friday."

Hallelujah! Praise be the Lord!

Bumming meals at Joe's Diner the remainder of the week. "Look Joe, I sold a story. I'll have the check Friday. I'll pay you up then."

Going home and writing like mad the rest of the week. Ecstasy. Not minding being hungry now. Just write. Write, write, write! The hell with the pain in your belly. You've got a sale, Johnny, kid. Get busy and give them another. Write a novelette. Next week we'll hit the jackpot.

And then *the* day. Friday. Wondering what time you should call around at the editorial office for the check. Not until after lunch, anyway. Don't look too anxious, kid. Just stroll in and say to the girl, "I happened to be in the neighborhood. I thought I'd drop by and pick up my check."

"They haven't been signed yet, Mr. Saxon."

Waiting. Three o'clock. Four o'clock. "No, Mr. Saxon they haven't been signed yet." Almost five o'clock. They close here at five, and they won't be open again until Monday. And you told the guy at the diner you'd pay him tonight. Christ! How am I going to *eat* over the week-end?

Five o'clock. "Look, miss, maybe they forgot to send it out front. Would you mind asking Mr. Morton . . ."

The girl looking bored. "I'll send a boy and have him ask the cashier, Mr. Saxon. Of course, you needn't worry. The checks will be mailed out in the morning, anyway."

Sure, they'll be mailed out, you dumb bell! And I

won't get mine until Monday. Some jerk's probably taking *you* out to dinner tonight. But not me!

And then that grand moment . . . that wonderful, precious second when a long white envelope is passed out through the receptionist's window. "Here it is, Mr. Saxon. They were just going to mail it out. Somebody forgot to tell them you were waiting."

Sneaking a look at it riding down in the elevator. Fifty bucks. Now! "In payment for all Serial Rights to *Contraband Carpses*. Please detach voucher before depositing."

Johnny sighed. The thoughts had flashed through his mind as he watched that lonely-looking kid go out of the office. He turned back to the blonde.

"Look, beautiful," Johnny murmured. "A tall, sort of distinguished-looking guy came up here just ahead of me. Baron von Elman. Whom did he go in to see?"

"You must be mistaken. He wasn't up *here*."

"You're certain?"

The girl nodded.

And then it hit Johnny. Of course! Baron von Elman must have spotted him, pretended to head for an elevator, and instead ducked out a side entrance of the building.

His brow furrowed. "Well, tell me this," he prompted. "Maybe he called somebody from outside. Do you remember anyone by that name calling somebody here?"

The girl consulted her note sheet. "I haven't any record of it, Mr. Saxon. Of course there were several calls, and the parties didn't always leave their names."

That was it, Johnny thought. The Baron was playing cagey!

"Who got calls just before I came up here?" he asked the girl.

Her forehead wrinkled in an effort at concentration. "Let me see . . . there was Mr. Clark, and Mr. Andrews, and Miss Leigh, and——"

"The hell with it!" said Johnny. He thought quickly. "I'll tell you . . . get me Miss Leigh." He remembered that he was supposed to call Kay, and as long as he was here he might just as well see her a moment. Not that he didn't *want* to see her, but he was afraid he might make another dinner date for tonight. And he had too much to do. Work and Kay Leigh didn't go together, as far as Johnny Saxon was concerned. Every time he thought of her a funny tingling ran through his veins.

The blonde was saying, "Miss Leigh is out to lunch."

"How long ago did she leave?"

"Just a few moments ago. They always use the back elevator."

Johnny frowned. Could von Elman have met Kay? Had he phoned her from outside the building? Why would he want to see her?

The idea did not make sense. Or . . . did it?

He grinned at the switchboard operator. "Well, thanks, baby. I'll be seeing you."

She gave him a smile and puckered her bright lips. " 'Bye," she said.

He rode the elevator to the lobby, located the phone booths and called the hotel. Moe Martin had just got in.

"How did you make out?" Moe asked.

"The Baron gave me the slip."

"I'll be damned!"

Then Moe added: "Look, call up Joe Rogers right away. He wants to see you. There was a slip at the desk when I came in."

"Anything else?"

"Not yet."

Johnny hung up. Outside, he hailed a cab. He was just swinging into the rear seat when he saw the small thin man headed toward the Mauser Building lobby. It was the Sontag Publications bookkeeper—Chick Clark—and he hurried along as though someone were chasing him.

Johnny Saxon vaguely remembered how worried Clark had been last night . . . worried because Les Hart, gangster, was loose somewhere in the city. He remembered the bookkeeper's remark about Jasper Ward trying to find somebody to take the rap for Sam Sontag's murder.

Clark acted almost as though *he* were going to be the fall guy!

Johnny slid into the seat and gave the driver the address of the Rogers Publishing Company.

CHAPTER EIGHTEEN

JOE ROGERS sat behind the highly polished desk in his oak-paneled office, his handsome, alert face solemn as he stared at the covers of his twenty-two magazines, that Hanna kept tacked on the wall of his office. He stood up, his tall lithe figure tense, and moved nervously up and down the room. He came back to the desk, started to pick up the phone, put it down again.

The door opened and Hanna came quietly into the room. She was wearing a knitted wool dress, and it molded the fine lines of her lovely figure.

"What's the matter, Pop?" she asked, seeing Joe's face.

He looked at her. And he thought, *She's the one I've done all this for. I've worked my guts out for six years, building up this house until it's one of the best pulp outfits in New York. And she's helped me. Every minute she's helped me, that swell kid.*

He said tensely, "Have you heard the news, pet?"

Hanna came across to the big desk. "What news?"

"That sneaking swine—George Howie. He's sold us out!"

Hanna stared, her cool green eyes worried. "How do you mean?"

"He's quitting. He's going over to the Sontag outfit. He's going to work for Jasper Ward."

"He told you that?"

Joe shook his head. "He shot off his mouth about leaving to one of the office boys. The kid tipped me off. I kicked Howie out on his fat can while you were out to lunch!"

Hanna said, "But, Joe, any editor has the right to leave——"

"That isn't all of it! I just found out the rest. Howie has been selling information about our books to the Sontag outfit for the past year. Getting *paid* for it. God knows what Jasper Ward knows about our plans for some of the news books, circulations, new authors we've got lined up and stuff." He stared at Hanna. "Do you realize what that means? Ward's in a position to undermine everything we've built up here. He can *ruin* us!"

Hanna came swiftly around the desk. Her slim hands were on his arms. Joe was trembling. "Honey," she said softly, "don't get so upset. You've fought your way up from the bottom. Nobody's going to lick you now. Jasper Ward's only a racketeer who doesn't know a thing about the publishing business. Sooner or later he'll go one step too far and have the police on his neck. Wait and see . . ."

"Yeah, wait!" Joe cried miserably. "We can't afford to wait. That chiseling outfit already has cut our throat. We're losing money every month. We're bleeding, baby. We're bleeding to death. And now, with that stinking louse Howie quitting just when we were working on those two new books . . ." He stopped, breathless, added: "You know what he did?"

Hanna shook her head.

"Howie's taken that new author—Philips—over to the Sontag outfit with him. Philips was doing the lead novel for our new detective book. Howie talked him into taking the story over to Sontag Publications. Offered him a half cent per word *higher rates!*"

"They've *never* paid decent rates at that house!"

"Of course not. But Philips fell for it. They'll give it to him on the first couple of stories, then cut him back to a half cent a word. But where does that leave us?" Joe ran his hand wearily through thick hair. "That new detective book goes to the printers Friday . . . and we haven't even got a lead novel! Or an editor either!"

Hanna bit her lower lip. "I can handle the magazine temporarily, until we get someone." Her eyes brightened. "How about Johnny Saxon? Maybe he'd have a story on hand we could use in a pinch."

Joe's arm went around her shoulder. "Baby," he said fondly, "I don't know what I'd ever do without you."

Hanna smiled. "I guess that goes double." She looked up at him, and her soft lips were crimson red, and he liked the smooth sweep of her high, immobile cheek bones. Her gaze dropped to his mouth. "I'm sorry the way things went Sunday morning, Joe. I was miserable all day, after you left."

His jaw again was hard. "That louse—A. A. Small! He phoned me again last night. He's still snooping around, and he's learned that I hated Sam Sontag's guts. He's still got a sneaking idea that I killed Sontag."

"No! Oh, Joe . . ." Hanna's eyes were worried. "You mean, he phoned you at Great Neck?"

He nodded.

"Did he mention anything about Sunday morning . . . that is, about you being at the apartment——"

Joe gave a brittle laugh. "That little punk would do anything. Of course he did. And I think Ann was listening in on the upstairs extension."

"Joe!"

"So what if she was!" He shrugged. "We had a scene last night. She kept saying she was going to Reno, and I asked her why the hell she didn't hurry up and get started. I've heard it for years. Sometimes I wish——"

Hanna's fingers touched his lips, held there. "Please, Joe!"

He smiled. "Okay, kid." He released her, moved across the room toward a clothes hanger. "Look, try to get hold of Johnny Saxon. I've been calling that guy all day. See if he's heard anything yet about Dulcy. Ask him about a lead novel for the new book." He paused, picked up a square, painted canvas that was resting against the wall. "Call Townsend and tell him this cover stinks. The coloring is awful. And tell him the hero is supposed to have two flaming automatics in his fists, not one.'

Joe had a custom-tailored black overcoat on his arm and a Homberg on the back of his well-shaped head. He leaned across the desk and gave Hanna a quick kiss. "Sweet, remind me to raise your salary. In fact, remind me to make you editorial director. I think I'll retire from this racket!" He grinned.

Hanna's eyes followed him somberly to the door. She asked suddenly, "Where are you going, Joe?"

"Over to see Jasper Ward. It's about time *somebody* told that rat that he's not going to get away with anything!"

Hanna's eyes were suddenly fear-filled. "Oh, Joe, be careful!" she cried. "You might lose your temper and do something . . ."

"Maybe I will!" Joe grinned, and went out.

She stood there, feeling shaken and weak. And she was thinking, *Please, God, don't let him do anything that will get him in trouble. He's impulsive. He'll act on the spur of the moment.*

It was very quiet in the room with Joe gone. It was very quiet and empty, like it always was without his alert personality.

Hanna leaned against the desk. She was trembling. "Joe," she whispered. "Joe, honey."

She wondered—she had thought of it often since the night of Sam Sontag's murder—if Joe Rogers, in sudden anger, could kill a man.

The phone was ringing.

The girl at the switchboard said, "Mr. Saxon to see Mr. Rogers."

"Send him down," said Hanna.

Johnny Saxon dropped his coat and hat on a chair and said, "Hi, Hanna. Where's Joe?"

"He just went out. He went over to see Jasper Ward."

Johnny's brows raised. "I get it. He's going to tell Ward where to head in."

"Exactly," agreed the girl. "And it's got me worried, Johnny."

Johnny studied the smooth planes of her face, her serious green eyes. He had known Hanna Carter for some time. He remembered the days when he'd been selling plenty of copy to this house. Joe Rogers and Hanna had always been swell. Many a Friday night they'd all stepped out together for a few cocktails. Johnny understood the situation that existed between Hanna and Joe. You don't miss a thing like that when you can read human nature the way Johnny Saxon could. As long as he could remember, he had realized that Hanna loved Joe. You could see it in the way she looked at him, the way her eyes brightened whenever he came into a room. It gave her a vitality that was appealing and beautiful. There weren't many girls like Hanna Carter, he thought.

Johnny sat down and tugged at his ear thoughtfully. "Joe's no fool," he told the girl. "I wouldn't worry about him. Ward's the guy who'd better start worrying—if he already hasn't started."

"Why?"

"Ward's on a spot. The police think he murdered Sontag. He's also frantic to find Dulcy—the only decent writer he's got on his magazines. On top of that, Les Hart, gangster, mysteriously crashes out of the Tombs. Ward pulled the strings on that one. The police are going to get wise to the fact before very long."

Hanna said, "I saw something about Les Hart in the papers. What would be Ward's reason for helping him to get out of jail?"

Johnny reached for a cigarette. The girl shook her head when he offered her one. "Now that Ward's a business man, a publisher"—Johnny grimaced—"he needs somebody to do his strong-arm work. And, whenever a smart-guy racketeer gets ideas about being a leading business man, he usually starts riding for a fall. I think that's what Jasper Ward's doing."

"Do you think he knows where Dulcy is, Johnny?"

He shook his head. "No, because he's offered me three grand to locate her."

"Johnny, I understand you were one of the last persons to see her. What's your idea about her disappearance? Do you think it's tied in with Sam Sontag's murder . . . I mean, do you think she's——" Hanna paused.

"Dead?" Johnny supplied.

She nodded.

"I'm positive she's very much alive."

Mention of Dulcy Dickens made Hanna remember what Joe had asked her to do. She told Johnny about the new detective book that they were bringing out, about their being in a spot for a lead short novel for the first issue.

Johnny said, "I've got a script at the office, something I once started that was supposed to be a book. I never finished it. I could wind it up—the whole thing—in a brief chapter." He grinned. "There's seven murders in the story. Would that do?"

"Perfect!" said Hanna. "Could you get the copy up here this afternoon? You can bang out the final chapter sometime this week."

Johnny picked up the phone, called the office of the *I Never Sleep* agency. Moe answered.

"I thought you were at the hotel," Johnny said in surprise.

"That damn kid," said Moe. "He never did bring the mail. I took a run down here to see what was what."

"Is he there now?"

"He just came in."

Johnny told him about the manuscript. "It's somewhere in that pile of stuff you call stories," Johnny said. "The title of it is *Tonight We Die.* Find it and shoot it right up here to the Rogers Publishing Company with Louie."

Moe gave a glad shout. "How much are we getting for it?"

"Never mind that," said Johnny. "Just get it up here." Then he asked, "Anybody looking for me before you left the hotel?"

"Captain Willis," said Moe worriedly.

Johnny swore. "That guy!"

He hung up.

Hanna looked relieved. "Johnny, you're swell. I'll put the story right through at our top rate . . ."

He waved his hand. "There's no rush." He frowned thoughtfully. "Getting back to this Jasper Ward business . . . what do you know about a man named Baron von Elman?"

"I've never heard of him."

"He's looking for Dulcy, too."

"Why?"

Johnny did not answer for a moment. Then he said, musingly, "I'm beginning to wonder. There's various angles, and they're kind of jumbled up in my mind. But I've picked up something. I've got to check on it first . . ." He snapped his fingers. "Which reminds me. I want to send a telegram. Mind if I use the phone?"

Hanna smiled. "Of course not. And charge it to the house." She started toward the door.

And Johnny exclaimed, "Hey, *wait* a minute. You don't have to leave the room. Besides, this will interest you."

She waited while he called Western Union.

A moment later, Johnny was saying, "The message

goes to the Chief of Police, New Orleans, Louisiana." He saw Hanna's eyebrows lift questioningly. "Here's the message: 'Interested in knowing if girl writer known here as Dulcy Dickens lives in your city. Please send full information collect'." Johnny gave his name, the address of the *I Never Sleep* agency, then hung up after the operator had checked on the phone number from which the call was being made.

"I don't get it," Hanna said, puzzled.

Johnny grinned. "I don't either—yet. It all depends on what reply I get to that wire."

She shook her head. "Johnny Saxon, you were always a great one for getting mixed up in things." Her eyes sobered. "You know, I wouldn't be at all surprised if you knew who murdered Sontag."

Johnny assumed a stage attitude of self-defense. "Hey *wait* a minute. I hope you don't think *I* did it!"

"I didn't mean it that way, Johnny. But I have an idea that probing mind of yours has *figured out* who might have killed him."

"Oh!"

"Well?"

Johnny's gray eyes flickered. "Now that you've asked, I'll tell you. Something happened today that gave me a crazy hunch. It's cockeyed as hell. And yet, I might be on the right track." He nodded slowly. "Ye-es, it could be possible. The only trouble is, I don't think I could prove in a thousand years that this person killed Sam Sontag."

Behind him, the voice said quietly, "You've been holding out on me."

Johnny spun.

Captain Nick Willis stood there, a derby pushed to the back of his bushy white hair, a cigar stuck in his heavy red face.

Johnny groaned. "That man's here again, mommie!" He added quickly, "I was just leaving."

"So was I," said the headquarters man. He took Johnny's arm and grinned broadly. "Let's leave together. Let's talk about murder, huh?"

CHAPTER NINETEEN

THREE HOURS LATER, standing at a bar on 42nd Street, Johnny Saxon leaned with his right arm around the captain's shoulder. Johnny was saying, "And so that's the way I've got it figured. You have somebody get up there to that publishing house and see what they can find out. Then, later, try what I said. Try that experiment."

Willis was feeling pretty good, and with good reason. Johnny had been buying him forty-five cent Scotch-and-sodas for the past hour.

"What about the dame?" Willis demanded. "What about that part of it?"

"Give me forty-eight hours," said Johnny. He had pushed his hat to the back of his head. He was sweating from talking so long and hard. "I told you I'm going to find Dulcy. But I've got to wait to hear something first. So give me that break."

The detective captain shrugged. "Okedoke. I'll give you until Wednesday, kid." His eyes flickered. "Until Wednesday morning. But if you don't come through, God help you! I'm getting sick and tired of the runaround I'm getting on this case."

A few moments later, Johnny left him. He was cold sober himself. He stared after Nick Willis' big figure in amazement, as the headquarters man walked down the street. Four dollars and a half worth of Scotch—and the man didn't even stagger!

Johnny went back to the hotel. The time was five o'clock Monday afternoon.

The time was 10:00 A. M., the day was Wednesday. In the drab, narrow-walled boarding-house room, Les Hart sat on the edge of the sagging metal bed and stared dully at the man facing him. Hart's face was dark with stubbly beard; his clothes looked like he'd been sleeping in them for several nights. His dark eyes were bloodshot.

He looked up at sleek, manicured Jasper Ward and said in a whining voice, "So what can I do? The cops have been on my tail for two days. I can't even go out to eat. I don't dare go to sleep. Christ, I'm going nuts! The first move I make they'll nab me and have me back in that louse-house, the Tombs. You know what happened down there one night?"

Ward's white, heavily powdered face was expressionless. "What?"

"I gave one of the screws two bucks to get me a couple of eggs and an extra blanket. You know, if you got dough you can send out for stuff. The rat brought me back two rotten eggs and a blanket off a guy that they'd just sent up the river for a ten-year stretch. The blanket was full of lice!"

Ward's strange, light-colored eyes were cool.

"You want to get out of town, don't you?" he asked.

"Sure. But how? With all the cops watching for me . . ."

"Shut up! I can arrange everything. I'll give you enough dough so that you can slip down to Mexico and lay low for a while——"

Hart's eyes brightened. "Thanks, Mr. Ward, that's great!"

"But first," Ward added quietly, "there's a little job to do——"

"Sure," the gangster said quickly, "anything you say, boss. Like I always said——"

"You know Joe Rogers, the publisher? I pointed him out to you a couple of times."

"Yeah, I know that guy. Louie knows him, too. That's how I remember——"

"All right, he's the one."

The flat, unemotional tone of Ward's voice brought a deep frown to Hart's forehead. "He's the one what?" he asked carefully.

"The one you're going to rub out."

Les tensed. "Christ! Not a guy like him!"

Ward's slim tapered fingers straightened the yellow silk handkerchief that was in the breast pocket of his form-fitting suit. He bent down, looked at his tie in the cracked glass of the dresser mirror. "Okay," he said easily, "okay. Let's forget the whole thing. Stay in this stinking room and rot, for all I give a damn." He started toward the door.

"Wait a minute!" Les cried. "Now, listen, I want to play ball with you——"

Ward's slender body swung around. His built-up heels clicked against the bare floor. "Well?" he snapped.

"Okay, boss," Hart murmured. "Anything you say."

Ward gave directions in his smooth, low voice. "Here's the set-up," he said. "I've already called Joe Rogers. I suggested that at noon today he meet me across the street from his office at the City Grill. You know where that is—right on Forty-second Street. I told him I'd been thinking over a few things and that maybe I'd had the wrong slant on this publishing racket. Told him I wanted to have a talk with him, and maybe we could straighten things out."

Hart's lined, bearded face looked up hopefully. "Can you?"

Ward's lip curled. "No! He's been getting in my hair. And he's the kind of lug who never knows when to quit. And so—he's got to go."

"Okay." Les sighed.

"Now you be there by that grill at exactly noon. Forty-second Street is jammed at that time of day. Carry some kind of bundle over your arm to conceal the gat. There's nothing to it, kid. Let him have it when he comes across the street. Scram into the crowd, duck around the corner of Third Avenue and I'll have Eli parked right there with the Packard. You can pull a fade easy as hell."

They discussed the plans further. Ward stepped toward the door, paused, picked a piece of thread from his pin-striped suit. "Eli will bring you around to meet me —later. I'll give you the dough, have everything arranged for you to meet some friends from St. Louis, and you'll be on your way. Easy, huh?"

Les Hart nodded slowly. "All right," he said. He sat there staring at the door after the dapper racketeer had gone out.

Five minutes later, from one of a number of phone booths in a drugstore on Fourth Avenue, Jasper Ward called police headquarters.

"This is a friend," he said quietly, holding a handkerchief over the mouthpiece. The handkerchief smelled of jasmine. "At exactly twelve o'clock noon today there will be a shooting near the City Grill, on Forty-second Street. I thought . . ."

"Hey, what *is* this?" demanded the desk sergeant.

". . . I thought," repeated Jasper Ward, "you might like to know."

He hung up, stepped casually from the booth and two minutes later was riding a cab uptown. He felt that his morning hadn't been wasted. With one deft stroke, he was eliminating Joe Rogers, at the same time making certain that there would never be any trail to himself.

Les Hart would shoot and kill Rogers. Until that murder happened, the police would not know who was going to be killed or who was going to do it. But the moment the shooting occurred, they'd swoop down on the murderer and kill *him.* He could almost see the headlines:

"MAD DOG KILLED BY POLICE IN DARING DAYLIGHT SHOOTING"

The newspapers did not say exactly that. In fact, the thing did not even rate a banner. But there was a small item on the first page of the early afternoon papers, and it said:

GANGSTER KILLED IN DARING POLICE TRAP

> Les Hart, New York gangster who recently escaped from the Tombs, was captured and killed today in a daring gun battle staged by detectives near the City Grill on East Forty-second Street.
>
> Hart was spotted loitering in a doorway by two headquarters plain-clothesmen. When the gangster was accosted, he swiftly drew an automatic and started shooting. Only through the quick action of the detectives was the man stopped before he might have killed innocent bystanders. The detectives had closed in with their guns held ready. Hart's body was riddled with bullets. Women cried in horror as he slumped to the sidewalk . . .

Johnny had the newspaper spread out on the battered desk of the *I Never Sleep* agency. He had been reading the news item to Moe.

Moe stood there with amazement creasing his round, sad face. Overgrown Louie Hart, his head held in his hands, sat across the room, his heavy shoulders slumped, his dark eyes red-rimmed. It was Louie himself who had brought in the newspaper just a few moments ago, dumbly pointing to the news item about his own brother. He just sat there now, holding his head, swaying a little. Tears stained his cheeks.

Johnny said thoughtfully, "It's too pat. There's more to it than is here in the paper."

"What do you mean?" Moe wanted to know.

"Les Hart was too smart to be hanging around on a busy street. He'd been hiding out the past few days. Why should he suddenly appear now . . ."

The phone was ringing.

Johnny jumped, made a grab for it. All morning he'd been sitting here in the office, waiting for a call. There had been no answer to his telegram to New Orleans. There had been no reply to the Lost and Found ad placed in the *Times*. Johnny was getting worried. Nick Willis had given him until today to find Dulcy . . .

He said, "Yes?" nervously as he picked up the receiver.

"Johnny? Johnny Saxon?"

It was Joe Rogers. He sounded excited.

"Yes?" Johnny prompted.

"Did you see the papers?"

"You mean . . . about that gangster, Les Hart?"

"Yes!" exclaimed Rogers. "Christ, you know what I figured out, Johnny?"

"What?"

"Jasper Ward called me this morning. Wanted to make a deal. Asked me to meet him across the street at the City Grill at noon. You know, right away I had a hunch. I said to Hanna, 'Honey, I'm going to wait . . .' "

Johnny sat up tensely. "I get it. I get it. How about this: Jasper Ward had you put on the spot. He had Les Hart planted there waiting for you to come out at noon hour. At the same time, Ward must have called the police and told them there was going to be a shooting. That's why those dicks were right there. And they saw Hart and he spotted them. He got panicky and drew a gat. So they let him have it."

"Exactly!" cried Joe.

"You're lucky, Joe damned lucky!"

Louie Hart's bloated face had raised from his hands. He had been listening to the telephone conversation intently. Now a peculiar expression came to his dark face and he stood up. He was trembling. He started to sweat. He felt the bulge of the automatic in his coat pocket, and he was thinking. *He killed Les. Jasper Ward killed my brother!*

He edged toward the hall door, a peculiar expression in his wild eyes. Johnny was busy talking. Moe was listening too. Neither one of them saw Louie go out . . .

Johnny hung up and said, "Where in hell's that kid?"

Moe, puzzled, stared around. "He was just here a minute ago."

The phone was ringing again. Johnny nervously scooped it up.

"This is Willis. What have you heard? Anything?"

"I've been waiting," said Johnny tensely. "I expect to hear something this afternoon sure. I sent another wire."

"You damn well better hear something," said Willis. "The Peanut's on my tail."

"You mean A. A. Small?"

"Yeah, him. He wants some action . . . About that other business. We've made a check. I think you might be right. We've got everything set. Jasper Ward hasn't been up there at the Sontag office all day. Now would be the time."

"Do you want me to make the call, Nick?"

There was silence on the wire for a moment. Then: "Okay, then call me back. I've got plenty of men planted around there right now."

"I'll call you in a couple of minutes," said Johnny.

He hung up, looked at Moe, cleared his throat, and said, "How does this sound?" And then he said, " 'This is Jasper Ward speaking.' "

Moe jumped. "Christ! Don't scare me like that. You sound just like him!"

"Swell, said Johnny, and picked up the phone again. He called a number, gave a name said, "This is Jasper Ward," in a tone that said Jasper Ward was plenty sore about something. Then added: "Bring over the books. *All* of them. *Get here right away!*"

"Yes, sir!" the thin, somewhat frightened voice answered quickly.

Johnny hung up, waited a moment, then he called Captain Willis, at headquarters.

"This is Johnny," he said. "Okay."

"Where'll I find you later?" asked the detective captain.

"Right here—unless I hear something. Then I'll leave word for you."

He hung up, waited a moment, then called the Palace Towers. He gave his name. "Have there been any messages for me?" He waited.

Moe had been listening without saying a word. Now his face showed amazement. "You sound like something was going to happen!" he exclaimed.

"Let's hope so," Johnny said.

The hotel clerk said, "Call Watkins nine-nine-three-four-five. A gentleman called and left that number. He said to tell you he had found Kiki.

Johnny clutched the phone. "He did!"

His hand was trembling as he jotted down the telephone number. He hung up again. He jumped up and gave a shout. "Wow!"

Moe stared at him worriedly. "You're getting excited," he said.

Johnny jumped back to the desk again, called the number that the hotel clerk had given him. Shortly, a man's voice said, "Hello?"

Johnny said, "This is the party who had the ad in the N. Y. *Times*. You called me at the Palace Towers. About the dog . . ."

"Yes," said the man's voice on the wire. "Could you come down here?"

"Where?" Johnny was tense.

"Christopher Street." He gave a street number. "That's in the Village, you know."

Johnny said, "I'll be right down," and hung up, and tried to control his excitement. "The Village!" he yelled, grabbing Moe and hugging him. "That would be it. That would be the logical place! Oh, gosh!"

Moe shook his head worriedly. "I hope you're feeling all right," he said solicitously.

Someone was knocking at the door. Moe answered it. He came back with a yellow envelope in his hand. "Telegram," he said to Johnny. "The kid says it's two bucks—collect."

Johnny pulled bills from his pocket. He handed Moe three singles. "This is my day," he said happily. "This is Johnny Saxon's day to howl." He ripped open the wire.

Moe shook his head, put one of the one dollar bills in his pocket, located a dime in his vest, and went back to pay the messenger boy.

Johnny was reading the wire. It was quite long.

"I'm a dope," he said as he stared at the message. "I should have thought of that before!"

"Thought of what?"

"Her name, of course. It's Dulcy Beaumont. It says so right here in the telegram!"

"I thought it was Dulcy Dickens?" said Moe.

"That's just a pen-name, don't you see? Dulcy Beaumont is her *real* name. This Jean Beaumont must have been her grandfather. He died about 1900. I looked it up last night . . ."

"What the hell are you talking about?"

Johnny was excited. He was almost dancing.

"I'll tell you later, Uncle. I think it's going to be a long story." He started hurriedly toward the door.

"What about those cops?" said Moe.

"I'll phone Willis later. You wait here in case anyone calls. I'll phone you back."

He raced out. He caught a cab to the Village. Fifteen minutes later he was talking to the man who had seen Kiki.

He was a short, quiet-looking man who said he was janitor of the apartment building to which Johnny had come.

"It's Apartment 5-A," said Johnny's informer. "I'm pretty sure about the dog. It answers to Kiki, all right. I tried it with other names, and that's the only one that worked."

"And it's a white poodle?"

The janitor nodded.

Johnny handed him a ten-dollar bill. "I'll go up alone," he said.

On the fifth floor, he located the apartment door. 5-A. The door was painted white, and there was a little bronze knocker.

He knocked twice and started praying.

Then the door opened, and she was standing there.

He saw her small, radiantly beautiful face. He saw her lustrous green eyes. Her lips were still the same burning red. She was wearing a brushed wool slipover sweater that molded her firm sharp breasts.

"Dulcy!" he cried.

She looked at him, staring. Her lip was quivering, and she rushed forward to grasp his hands.

"*Shonny!*" she said in her low soft voice.

CHAPTER TWENTY

LOUIE HART stood in the foyer entranceway of Jasper Ward's apartment and glared at the well-dressed racketeer. There was a small automatic in Louie's fist, and his flushed face was bloated with anger.

"I've always wanted to kill somebody," Louie said in his low husky voice. "But I've never wanted to kill any guy like I want to kill you!" He moved slowly forward, his pin-pointed eyes on Ward's dapper, almost womanish figure.

"Now look, kid," said the racketeer worriedly, "let's talk this over. What's wrong with you?"

"You damn well know what's wrong with me, punk!"

"Listen——"

"You killed my brother. You killed Les." Louie's voice rose shrilly. "You sent him up there to get Joe Rogers and then you called the cops. You stinking louse! I'm going to kill you for that!"

Sweat stood out on Louie's dark features; his eyes held an inhuman stare. He kept coming forward, across the foyer, into the living room with the rich, cream-colored leather furniture. Over by the windows, the built-in radio was playing softly. "*It was Fiesta down in Mexico. . .*" Artie Shaw playing *Frenesi.* It was good. It went nice with the well-chosen furnishings of the room.

Ward's strange, light-colored eyes narrowed. His thin sharp face was tense. He kept backing up, one hand in the pocket of his maroon-red bath-robe. "Christ, kid, somebody's been handing you a line. Les and I were pals. You know how it was . . ."

The gun in Louie's big fist never wavered. He was laughing, and it wasn't pleasant. "I'm going to give it to you right in the guts. I want to see you squirm. It's going to be funny as hell watching you die." He took another jerky step forward.

"Listen,——" Ward started.

"Don't give me that crap!"

"I've tried to tell you——"

"Here it comes, rat!" said Louie. He stopped walking. His fingers tightened on the butt of the gun.

Ward fired through the pocket of his bathrobe. He was thinking, *The punk really was going to kill me!*

The slug caught Louie in the mouth, traveled upward into his brain. He fell to the rich tan rug and blood started making a crimson stain beside his head.

Sight of the blood froze Ward with horror. He recoiled. He screamed, "Mike!"

But the Filipino house man had already come running into the room at the sound of the shot. Ward motioned jerkily to the motionless figure on the floor, and said shrilly, "We've got to get him *out* of here!"

Mike shook his head sadly. "No doing now. Somebody maybe seeing you."

Ward started to sweat. His mouth twitched. Suddenly the full realization of the predicament he was in became obvious. How would he ever get the body out of this apartment house? How would he ever explain Louie Hart's disappearance? There would be someone who had seen the dumb bastard come up!

He saw what one single lead slug had done. He saw everything crashing around him—the publishing business, the distributing firm, his apartment. The police would come and question him. They'd have the body. They'd have him dead to rights.

"Christ!"

He looked at Mike and screamed, "Pack my bags! Pack everything! Hurry!"

Ward's manicured hand rubbed dazedly over his face. His thoughts were jumbled. But one thing pounded through his brain. He couldn't get that dead body out of here. So he'd get out *himself.*

Twenty minutes later he was on his way to Grand Central.

It was Wednesday night, and it was snowing again. Throughout Manhattan, office buildings poured clerks and stenographers and office boys into the street.

Kay Leigh signalled a cab and headed down town. She looked tall and slim and lovely in a tailored black coat. Her lips shone orange-red as the cab passed the frequent street lights.

Washington Square looked like a white-clad village

common in the country. Snow clung to the trees. It formed a soft virgin blanket on the ground. Tomorrow it would be gray and dirty.

The taxicab finally arrived at the apartment house on Christopher Street. Kay rode the elevator to the fifth floor. A second later she was ringing the buzzer of 5-A.

Johnny Saxon opened the door. His pleasant gray eyes were smiling.

"Hi, baby. Welcome to the homecoming!"

Kay stared.

Johnny led Kay into the living room. Dulcy was there, looking young and sweet in the brushed wool sweater and a close-fitting skirt. She came across the room and put her arms around slender Kay Leigh. "Shonny has told me everything," she said brightly.

Kay looked at him. Her flashing black eyes were puzzled. "Then you knew?"

Johnny nodded. "Sunday afternoon, when you tried to get me half plastered," he said grinning. "I didn't know—but I guessed. Only I couldn't remember what it was I guessed until a little while ago." He shrugged. "I won't hold it against you, beautiful."

Kay bit her lower lip. "I had an idea you came down to see me only to ask questions. All along I had the feeling you suspected something." She held his gray eyes a moment, added: "You see, Baron von Elman had told me you trailed him last Saturday night. I had a hunch——"

Johnny smiled. "He told me right at the beginning that he'd been to see you. He was neither an agent nor a writer. I got to wondering about that. I did a little checking up. I found out that, on the side, you acted as an agent for a few good writers. You handled their stuff."

Kay had slipped out of her coat. She was wearing something green and closefitting. Johnny remembered how firm and lithe her legs had looked in the sheer lounging negligee.

She said, "I had a feeling things were going to blow up at Sontag Publications. Jasper Ward and Sam were forever fighting. A girl has to have a job." She gave Johnny a provocative look. "I was going to become a full-time literary agent if I lost my job."

"You're all right," Johnny admitted. He saw Dulcy's small, shapely figure heading toward the kitchen. Kiki was barking out there about something. "You spotted the real masterpieces that were behind Dulcy's stories. You figured you could get a writer like her into the slicks in no time."

Kay nodded. "She's a genius, no doubt about it."

"Where did von Elman enter into it?"

"I'd met him once. I knew he was quite an authority on manuscripts and books. I had him look over some of Dulcy's stuff. We learned that her grandfather was a well-known French writer—Jean Beaumont. She must have gotten her talent from him."

She frowned. It made her lovely mouth the more sultry. "How did you find out about Dulcy? I thought I had her well hidden here, Johnny."

He explained. "I stepped in that dish beneath your kitchen sink. There was some salmon in that bowl, and you said you had a cat. I never saw a cat yet that left even a scrap of fish remaining in a food dish. Later, in the bedroom"—his lean face colored slightly—"I saw that you didn't even have a cat. I figured that Dulcy must have been there with the poodle. Kiki. You had given the pooch something to eat there in the kitchen."

"And I thought you were drunk!" said Kay.

"I was. I was feeling pretty goddamned splendid." He met her dark eyes. "I'd like to try it again sometime when we have more time."

Kay nodded toward the kitchen. "Who's out there?"

"My partner."

Just then Moe Martin appeared in the doorway. His round, usually sad face was now wreathed in a happy smile. In his left hand he held a plate; in his right, a large sandwich. He was munching on the sandwich and smiling at Dulcy who clung to his arm.

Dulcy said, "Isn't he cute, Shonny?"

"He's cute and he's always hungry," said Johnny.

Kay asked: "Who else is coming down here?"

"Everybody," Johnny told her. "It's going to be quite a party. We might even have a policeman or two."

"You mean——" Kay's eyes clouded. "About Sam Sontag? You've got that figured out too?"

"I think so. I'm waiting to hear from Nick Willis."

The others started arriving a few moments later.

There was tall, steely gray-haired Baron von Elman. He looked suspiciously at Johnny Saxon and had little to say. He drew Kay Leigh to one side and started talking rapidly in a low voice.

Johnny smiled to himself. The apartment buzzer was ringing, and he hurried to answer the door.

It was handsome Joe Rogers and Hanna, looking bright and gay, as though they might have just come from their own church wedding.

"Hi, kids," said Johnny. He steered them across the living room. "Here she is. Dulcy!"

Joe Rogers stared.

Hanna, her cool green eyes studying Dulcy's fresh and lovely face, exclaimed, "Isn't she a darling!"

Johnny said, "This is supposed to be a celebration, and we haven't even got a drink."

"The hell we haven't!" said Rogers, looking at Johnny. "I've got a couple bottles in the car."

"My God!" put in Moe. "Somebody's liable to steal it down there!"

By the time they had opened the second bottle, they were all old friends. Everybody was talking at once.

Nick Willis arrived. His face was somber. He looked tired.

Someone said, "God! I forgot. One of us is a suspect in a murder."

And Johnny said quietly, "Maybe not." He looked at the white-haired detective-captain. "How did you make out, Nick?"

Willis had dropped wearily into an armchair. He dropped his coat to the floor beside him. He was still wearing his derby.

Joe Rogers and Hanna were seated very close together on the divan. Baron von Elman, looking sore about something sat stiffly on a straight-backed chair across the room.

Kay and Johnny were perched up on a table, books crowded back against the wall behind them. Kay's long slim legs, lovely in sheer silk, swung beneath the table, and Moe Martin stood leaning against the wall watching them. Johnny gave him a sharp look. Dulcy was curled up in a chair near Moe. Her sweet face was bright and eager. From time to time she looked over at Johnny and smiled coquettishly.

Willis said, "Well, kid, he was the one. We followed him when he left the office. Later, we nailed the guy just ready to hop a Florida express. He had all the books with him. He was taking a powder. We told him we were taking him back to see Jasper Ward, and he damn near went nuts. He told us the whole story."

"He killed Sontag, then?"

The detective captain nodded. "Ward thought Sam was chiseling on the profits. It wasn't Sam at all. Sam did a little checking up and found out the truth. The books were in a mess. He was being gypped out of thousands . . ."

Kay was staring. "You sound as though you were talking about Chick Clark, the bookkeeper," she said.

Willis nodded grimly.

"But how did you prove it?"

"We didn't," Johnny said. "We didn't have any proof at all that Clark was the murderer. But I had a hunch." He looked at Kay and said meaningly, "That night he came down to your apartment. He was scared. He was scared as hell because Les Hart was out of jail. He knew Jasper Ward was going to try and find the real murderer. I phoned Chick this morning and pretended I was Jasper Ward. Told him I wanted to see the books right away. Clark knew the jig was up. He got panicky and tried to skip town——"

"So did somebody else," said Willis.

Johnny shot a glance. "Who?"

"Jasper Ward himself."

"The hell he did!"

"Because we happened to have plain-clothes men watching railroad stations, we were able to nab him. We had a tip-off from some tenant in Ward's building that there'd been a shooting. So when we got back there we found this kid, this Louie Hart——"

It was Johnny Saxon's turn to show surprise. "Louie?"

"Him," said Willis flatly. "He went up there to bump Ward off, and instead got a slug himself." He sighed. "So that about cleans things up." He spread his big hands. "The one guy we were ready to pin the rap on for murder didn't kill Sontag at all. We figured it musta been Ward. And it wasn't him at all. Ain't it funny the way things sometimes work out?"

Willis looked across the room at Dulcy Dickens. "Is this the cutie everybody's been looking for?" He stood up, and exclaimed, "Christ, isn't it about time somebody offered me a drink?"

Later—Johnny was feeling pretty good, and it was probably because of this that he decided to tell them now, though he had not intended to reveal it tonight—Johnny got everybody's attention and said, "Dulcy's got something to say to you." He went over and put his arm around the girl's shoulder. "Tell them about it, baby."

Dulcy's green kitten eyes were suddenly serious and level.

"It's about my stories," she said in her low, soft voice.

Everyone was looking at her.

"You see," she said, "they are not really mine."

Joe Rogers gasped. "They're *not!*"

The girl shook her head.

"Good Lord, and I was going to publish them!"

Baron von Elman glowered even more darkly. But he said nothing.

Johnny said, "Go on, Dulcy."

She looked at Johnny. Her emotional face was somber. "You explain to them about the manuscripts, Shonny."

Johnny said, "It all centers around Dulcy's trunks. Kay had her baggage checks. She gave them to the Baron, and he was supposed to get the trunks." Johnny smiled grimly, flicking a glance at the tall book-dealer. Before bringing the trunks here, he took them up to his place, opened them, sneaked a look at some of Dulcy's manuscripts." Johnny smiled. "I took the liberty of reading part of one that he kept for himself, before bringing the trunks down here. I read it at the Baron's desk."

Von Elman glared.

Johnny continued, "Dulcy probably has a hundred

thousand dollars' worth of manuscripts in her trunks, which she brought from New Orleans. They are in French. They are the stories that she has been rewriting into English and selling in New York. They are beautiful stories. They are terrific. Only thing wrong with them is . . . they are plagiarized!"

Everyone gasped. Moe Martin looked as though he had swallowed something sour. Perhaps he was thinking of his contract.

"Dulcy's grandfather," Johnny went on, "was a well-known French novelist. Jean Beaumont. Upon his death, he left all his manuscripts to Dulcy, here. The scripts were sent to her in New Orleans. Dulcy thought they were swell stories. So she transposed them into English."

"I didn't know," Dulcy said with lowered eyes. "I didn't know about this thing you call plagiarism."

Johnny looked at Baron von Elman and grinned. "The Baron, being an expert, realized the truth immediately. He wanted to get hold of those manuscripts, but he didn't want to pay what they were worth. He thought if he could find Dulcy, he would persuade her to sell them for a song. But if he wants them now, it's going to cost him plenty. And the Baron, I'm afraid, hasn't the money. In fact, the Baron is broke. Isn't it so, Baron?"

Baron von Elman suddenly picked up his hat and coat, glared at everybody, then stalked out.

Johnny had slid from the table and was standing beside Kay Leigh. He patted her arm and whispered, "Too bad, baby. You've lost your best client."

She gave him a warm, sultry look. "You can't blame a girl for trying."

Somebody suggested sending out for more liquor. Somehow, a little later, everybody was crowded out into the kitchen. Every time Johnny looked at Dulcy's young, sweet face, a tremor of emotion surged through him. If she wasn't such a kid . . .

A drink in his hand, he wandered back to the living room. He paused in the doorway as he saw Hanna and Joe Rogers, in each other's arms. He had not wanted to eavesdrop, but he couldn't help hearing Joe's husky words.

" . . . and so she's finally gone to Reno. It seems like I've waited for years, baby——"

"It was worth every minute of it, Joe."

"Yes. Every minute. Now I have you. Forever.

"Joe!"

He was holding her very close. They were a fine-looking couple together.

Johnny slipped back into the kitchen. "Let's all go some place," he said.

And then it was Thursday morning, and in the spacious room at the Palace Towers it was quiet and solemn. Moe Martin sat staring out the window. His face was very unhappy.

He turned and said to Johnny, "Jasper Ward was going to pay us three thousand dollars. But now he's in jail."

Johnny was standing at the dresser mirror knotting a polka dot blue tie.

"And," continued Moe dismally, "Baron von Elman was going to pay five grand. But he was going to pay out the dough he realized on Dulcy and the manuscripts. And now he won't get either. So that lets ***him*** out."

"Quite right," agreed Johnny.

"When is the room rent due again?"

"Saturday."

"Have we got any money left?"

"A couple of dollars," said Johnny brightly. "But why worry?"

"My God!" cried Moe. "What are we going to do . . ." Suddenly his eyes brightened. "How about Joe Rogers? How about that story you gave him?"

"They'll get around to sending out a check."

"Why not call them up?"

"I wouldn't think of it," said Johnny.

Moe groaned.

There was quiet a knock at the door.

It was Dulcy, looking young and lovely in a traveling outfit of delicate gray. Across the hall, a bellhop was just locking the door of her room. He bent down to pick up the luggage that he had set out in the hall.

"Shonny," Dulcy said softly, "I just came to say good-bye."

She came into the room. She shook hands solemnly with Moe. She turned back to Johnny. "I'll write to you sometime," she said.

He found it hard to talk. "So you're going back to New Orleans?"

She nodded. Her green eyes were a little misted.

"Well, good luck, kid," said Johnny. And then, on a sudden impulse, he said, "Do you mind if I kiss you on the forehead?"

She leaned toward him. His lips brushed her soft skin. He was thinking, *Why did she have to be such a kid?*

She turned away. She was crying softly . . .

Johnny stood there a long time staring at the closed door. Then he gave a sigh and moved toward the phone. Moe said:

"She sure was nice." He shook his head. "Too bad she didn't know that you aren't supposed to peddle stories that have once been sold."

"They were never sold before," said Johnny.

Moe stiffened.

"What do you mean?"

"I mean, everyone of those manuscripts she's got are originals. Stories written by her grandpappy and never published. They are masterpieces. They are probably worth a fortune. Jean Beaumont was another Du Maupassant."

Moe's face turned pale. He collapsed into a chair. "Oh, my God," he gasped. "And you let Dulcy go back to New Orleans!"

Johnny nodded. "I couldn't see that sweet kid getting gypped. I'm going to write her a letter when she gets home and tell her the truth."

Moe sat there rubbing his bald head sadly. "Something tells me," he muttered, "we're going to be hungry again."

Johnny picked up the phone. "How would you like to come down to Kay's to dinner with me tonight?"

He called the number.

THE END

TO THE READER

If you enjoyed this book, you will be glad to know that there are many others just as well written, just as interesting, to be had in the Fiction House Press Library.

You will find the Fiction House Press Library online at

www.FictionHousePress.com

www.ingramcontent.com/pod-product-compliance
Lightning Source LLC
LaVergne TN
LVHW090955080826
845145LV00003B/1012

* 9 7 8 1 6 4 7 2 0 5 8 8 1 *